"Travis, wait for me in the hall. I'll be done in a few minutes,"

Winnie said. She looked desperately toward the front of the lecture hall and saw that the TA had stopped grading papers.

"Oh, no," Winnie sighed, as the TA stormed up the aisle.

Travis knelt down next to her again.

"Travis, please."

"Okay, Win. I'll see you in a few minutes."

Winnie started to look back down at her exam, but Travis put a swift hand to her face, turned her toward him, moved in, and kissed her. It was a long intense kiss, right on the mouth, right in the middle of her midterm! Winnie's head reeled.

Don't miss these books
in the exciting FRESHMAN DORM
series

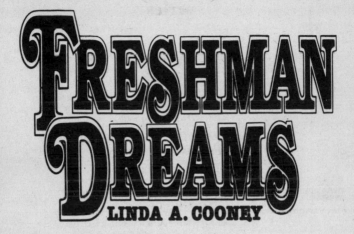

FRESHMAN DREAMS

LINDA A. COONEY

HarperPaperbacks
A Division of HarperCollinsPublishers

This is a work of fiction. The characters, incidents, and dialogues are products of the author's imagination and are not to be construed as real. Any resemblance to actual events or persons, living or dead, is entirely coincidental.

HarperPaperbacks   *A Division of* HarperCollins*Publishers*
10 East 53rd Street, New York, N.Y. 10022

Cover art by Tony Greco

First HarperPaperbacks printing: January 1991

Printed in the United States of America

HarperPaperbacks and colophon are trademarks of HarperCollins*Publishers*

1 0 9 8 7 6 5 4 3 2

One

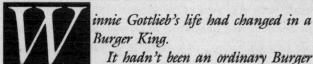**W**innie Gottlieb's life had changed in a Burger King.

It hadn't been an ordinary Burger King. It was a Burger King in Paris, France, which was furnished with little café tables and served sandwiches on baguettes.

Winnie had gone in for an old-fashioned hamburger and a Coke. Waiting in line, trying to pass herself off as a French student or a traveler from Rome, she had first laid eyes on him. His blond hair had rested on his shoulders. He'd been wearing faded French jeans, a soft collarless shirt, and the kind of open, loose vest she'd seen on so many Parisian guys since she'd arrived on her teen exchange earlier that summer. When he'd reached the register, just ahead of her, and dug in his pocket for change, he'd pulled out three tortoiseshell guitar pics along with his francs and his centimes.

The guitar pics had made Winnie think of music, how her Walkman had broken the first week she'd arrived in France, and how much she missed KJAC, the radio station from her small town of Jacksonville back home. That had made her think about how much she missed everything at home: shopping malls and baseball and awful American junk food. Most of all she missed her best friends, Faith and KC. Thinking of Faith and KC had made Winnie feel so overwhelmed by homesickness that when a Muzak version of a corny old rock song about mountains and rain had come over the Burger King speakers, she had burst into tears.

"S'il vous plaît?" the girl at the counter had prodded.

Winnie had stared through her tears, speechless for once in her life, while the boy with the long, blond hair had lingered at the counter in front of her, gathering napkins and straws.

"I can't believe it." Winnie had finally mumbled. "Even Muzak is sounding good to me. This is pathetic. What am I doing with my last summer before college? I'm so homesick. I want to go home."

And that's when he had turned around, ready to take his food to a table.

Winnie had taken one look at him and had wanted to throw her arms around his neck and weep. All her homesickness had disappeared as she stared into what seemed to be an all-American face: clear blue eyes, dimpled chin, straight-toothed smile—framed by long blond hair. Still, his hip European clothes made Winnie think he had to be Parisian. For about the hundreth time that summer, she cursed herself for not studying harder through all those years of high school French.

"*Oui?*" *the counter girl asked her.*

Winnie had been too distraught and distracted to place her order. She'd just stood speechless until he'd made a move to go past her. That's when she tried to give him room but ended up shifting in the same direction, so that they collided.

"*Excusez moi,*" *Winnie had whispered, her tears still wet and slipping down her cheeks. She'd half expected him to hear her American accent, roll his eyes, and storm away.*

Instead, he'd come to life, acting as if she were his oldest, dearest friend. "All right!" he'd cried in a raspy, subtly southern voice. "An American! My brain is working overtime, trying to get by in French, especially since I just came from Italy and Germany before that and, man, am I'm starting to get confused. I've been on the road for seven months, just me and my guitar, and I'm starting to feel like home is something you just write songs about. Isn't that the way it is? When you're home, all you want to do is leave, and when you're on the road, you miss home so much you think you'll die. It's all or nothing, man."

He had taken Winnie's breath away.

"Come sit with me, beautiful," he'd urged. "Talk to me. Tell me everything about you and I'll tell you everything about me and then I know we'll both feel great."

Winnie had done just that. She'd sat with him. She'd talked. She'd listened. And the whole time, she'd known that Travis Bennett was going to change her life.

"So, Winnie, how long has it been since you last saw Travis?" Faith asked.

"Five months, four days, and six hours."

"But who's counting."

"Very funny, KC. I can't believe I'm going to see him again!"

"Are you nervous?"

"AM I NERVOUS? Sure, I'm nervous. I'm insane, ready to jump out of my skin, demented. Why do you think I was so glad you two could come along with me on this ride?"

Faith turned around in the driver's seat and winked. "Because KC and I are so cool, calm, and collected."

Winnie leaned forward and clutched KC and Faith's shoulders. "Compared to me right now, a cage of monkeys is cool, calm, and collected."

The three best friends were heading away from their university dorms, toward the Springfield bus station on a foggy November day. Thanksgiving break was coming up. Midterms were around the corner. They were nearly halfway through their first semester at college, and Winnie's life had changed again.

"What time is Travis's bus supposed to get in?" asked Faith as she maneuvered the steering wheel of the borrowed university van. Her hair was swept back in a French braid, and she wore a long denim jumper with an old WESTERN DRAMA FESTIVAL sweatshirt, an antique scarf, and cowboy boots.

"Twelve-fifteen." Winnie was in the backseat, shifting and wiggling so frantically that her long earrings jangled and the six bracelets she wore on each wrist clanked. She pitched forward to check her short, spiky hairdo in the rearview mirror. "We're going to make it, aren't we? Please, please say yes, Faith."

"Fear not, Win. We'll make it." Faith patted the dashboard. "Thanks to the trusty U of S day-care van."

"The trusty, sticky day-care van," cracked KC. She put down her Intro to Business book for a moment and peeled a piece of soggy cracker off her seat belt. Although KC sat tall in her usual dress-for-success blazer, skirt, and little bow tie, she looked unusually relaxed. Her gray eyes sparkled and her dark hair curled more softly than usual around her beautiful face.

"Come on, KC," Faith teased. "You always talk about how important it is to have connections. Well, I have day-care connections." As an independent study project, Faith was directing her own experimental production of *Alice in Wonderland* with a cast made up of freshmen, plus two University of Springfield day-care kids. "That's how I got the van."

"Sounds okay to me." KC laughed. "I'm just along for the ride. I really needed a break from studying all morning. Plus I love riding downtown on upholstery covered with cookie crumbs."

"KC, you're suddenly acting much too mellow," said Winnie. "What happened to the overachieving, overly intense, sorority hopeful we used to know?"

KC held up her textbook. "She's still here. I guess I'm just in a better mood."

"Well, don't be. It just makes me even more nervous." Winnie shifted in the backseat. "Anyway, I for one am eternally grateful for this ride—cookie crumbs or no cookie crumbs. I'm delighted, wildly relieved, insanely and totally grateful for the rest of my life. I would never have made it in time if I'd had to walk. Or run."

Faith grinned. "You're welcome."

"Thanks."

The van cruised past the fancy shops on the Springfield Strand toward the older, funkier part of downtown. Striped awnings and well-dressed windows turned into brick warehouses and parking lots.

"I'm even more grateful," Winnie chattered on, "because my life is beginning to feel about as surreal as a production of *Alice in Wonderland*. Did I tell you two about the dream I had last night?"

Faith shook her head.

KC smiled. "But I'm sure you will, Win."

"You're right," Winnie breathed, leaning forward again. "It was more of a nightmare actually. Okay, I dreamed that I had to race out of Hermann's Western Civ class to meet Travis's bus. I was trying to get downtown, running faster than I'd ever run in all my ten million exercise jogs, except that I wasn't getting anywhere because the sidewalks kept moving the other way. Isn't that weird?" Winnie slowed down for a moment. "Are you two following this?"

Faith nodded.

"Every word," KC assured her.

"Good." Winnie rested her chin on the back of the front seat. "So finally this little French car pulled up to give me a lift. I got in and who do you think was driving?"

"Tweedledum," Faith suggested.

"No!"

"Who?" asked KC.

"Professor Hermann! Except that he was dressed like me, wearing purple tights and a little black miniskirt."

Faith cringed.

KC laughed.

"Believe me, it wasn't a pretty sight." Winnie took a breath. "So Hermann started quizzing me on the Greeks and the Etruscans and all the stuff that's going to be on our killer Western Civ midterm, and I was trying to think of the answers when I looked at him again. Only guess who he'd suddenly turned into?"

Faith and KC shrugged.

"TRAVIS!"

"Really?" Faith gasped.

"Really." Winnie nodded. "It gets even weirder, because then he turned into none other than Josh Gaffey!"

The light turned to yellow and Faith slammed the brakes, reaching across to protect KC, while

KC and Winnie reached out to steady themselves. After the jolt, all three girls were silent.

"What about Josh?" Faith finally asked, looking at Winnie in the rearview mirror.

"Yeah, what's up with Josh?" KC asked in a soft voice.

"Ugh." Winnie flopped back on the seat and kicked her boots, so that the small bells strapped around them jingled. "This is the ultimate Winnie Gottlieb screwup. I mean, I meet Josh my first week at college, when I'm still flipped out and madly in love with Travis. And now I'm about to see Travis again just when I'm totally freaked out and madly in love with Josh!"

The light turned green and Faith stepped on the gas. KC flicked on the radio, but the campus station's broadcast of the U of S basketball game didn't help distract Winnie. She lay on the backseat and remembered every crazy, agonizing detail of the mess she was in with Travis Bennett and Josh Gaffey.

During orientation week, Winnie had fallen instantly for funny, thoughtful Josh. But she'd blown it by drinking way too much and passing out in his room, which had created major weirdness and misunderstandings. Josh lived in the same dorm as Winnie, right down the hall. They saw each other often, but there had been more misunderstandings as the semester wore on, and Winnie had begun to doubt that things would ever work out. Then, just when a big date was planned between her and Josh, Travis popped back into Winnie's life. Travis had phoned just as Winnie was leaving for her date, and of course motor-mouthed Winnie had talked on and on and on. By the time she'd hung up and rushed to meet him, Josh was gone. And Josh hadn't spoken to her since.

Winnie suddenly sat up as the Springfield bus station came into view. Just seeing the plain brick walls and the sign with the running greyhound made her blood churn and her face flush.

"We're here," Faith announced.

"I can't believe all this is happening!" Winnie cried.

"Winnie, stay cool for once," KC warned.

As Faith strained to parallel park the van, KC turned around to calm Winnie. "What I can't believe is that you and Travis had such a hot and heavy romance over the summer, then he left to go travel some more and you thought he'd forgotten you."

Winnie searched madly through her carpetbag, grabbed a messy sack of makeup, and began making frantic dabs at her face. "What I can't believe is that he really *hadn't* forgotten me, that he just sent all his letters to the wrong address. I'm so used to having guys dump me that I still can't believe it didn't happen again." She collapsed. "How do I look?"

Faith turned off the van's engine and pulled out the key. She and KC turned around to stare at Winnie. "You look great."

"Winnie," KC insisted, "just don't get carried away again."

Faith pointed a finger. "KC's right. Things are going so well for you now. You're doing well in your classes. Remember how nuts things were when we first got here?"

"I remember, Mother Faith."

"You kept messing up and going to extremes," KC reminded her.

"I remember, Sergeant KC."

KC frowned. "We just don't want you doing that again."

"Don't worry. I won't. I promise. I've learned."

The girls got out. Faith locked up, while KC put change in the meter and Winnie respiked her hair. Then Faith and KC locked arms with Winnie, and the three of them strode together into the bus station.

Inside the station was a collage of video games, candy machines, old cigarette smoke, gray lockers with the orange keys attached, and TV chairs where people put coins in to watch television. Winnie stood in the middle of the station while all that chaos swirled around her. She scanned schedules and advertisements with blurry eyes until she heard a rumble and the hiss of high-powered brakes.

"There's his bus!" Winnie screamed as a big, silver bus pulled up. She had no reason to be sure it was Travis's bus, except that she felt it with all her heart. Sure enough, as soon as she ran outside through double glass doors she saw the destination sign on top of the arriving bus. *Seattle/Denver.* The door swung open and the bus driver stepped out to open up the luggage storage underneath.

Winnie stood there, her heart pounding, breathing in all that smoke and exhaust, while KC and Faith slowly joined her and people began to climb off the bus. There were kids, tourists, grandmas, college students. They found their luggage, rubbed their eyes, and wandered away.

Winnie bit her lip. She stared and waited. Fear ran through her as she felt KC and Faith move closer, waiting for the famous Travis to appear. They waited and waited. Winnie's heart slowed down.

Finally Faith spoke. "Maybe he took another bus."

"Maybe he missed this one."

"Are you sure, Winnie, this is the right bus?"

The bus driver was taking the very last bags out from the cargo area. No one else was getting off. Winnie went dull inside, as if someone had let all the life out of her. She felt as if she'd been seduced into high expectation, only to be dumped once again. She started to head back into the station.

At that very moment there was a *crash* from the rear of the bus. Through the tinted glass a figure could be seen rising from the very back seat.

Winnie spun around. Her eyes were fixed. Her hands folded and unfolded nervously, and then she took a tiny step toward the bus in tentative anticipation.

The figure inside the bus froze. Then suddenly he was at one of the windows, knocking with his fist and waving. "WINNIE! YOU'RE HERE! MAN, YOU LOOK BEAUTIFUL!"

Faith and KC both looked at each other.

Winnie brought her hands to her mouth as Travis left the window and hurriedly climbed over another seat on the bus. There he picked up several awkward-looking cases and flung them ahead of him as he made his way down the narrow aisle. By the time he got to the open doorway, it sounded like a small building had collapsed. Faith and KC stood mesmerized.

"WINNIE!" he shouted again, laughing as he stepped off the bus and looked at her. His blond hair hung to his shoulders. His face was bright, his eyes hopeful, his expression full of joy. Despite the cold, he was outfitted in sandals, jeans, a sleeveless T-shirt, and a vest that flapped open. In one hand he held a backpack and an acoustic guitar in a metal case, and in the other, two big electric basses in zippered sacks.

Travis bumped his way down the last steps of the bus, put down the bass guitars, leapt a few steps, swung his arms around Winnie, and hugged her, managing to hang onto his acoustic guitar case and backpack.

"Travis," Winnie whispered.

"Win! Beautiful Win."

Winnie just stood there, letting herself be enveloped by five months worth of missing him and wondering and hurting so much when she thought he'd forgotten her. Finally she raised her arms and reached around his warm, familiar back. As soon as she did, she remembered a hundred other embraces from another time and felt that her life was about to be totally changed again.

Two

....

"I love a good scandal," Dash Ramirez remarked.

"I love a good story," Lauren said.

"I just hope you two have your facts straight," barked Greg Sukamaki, editor of the U of S *Weekly Journal.* "That's all that matters to me."

It was later that afternoon, and Faith's roommate, Lauren Turnbell-Smythe, was standing shoulder to shoulder with her new writing partner and maybe boyfriend, Dash Ramirez. Dressed in army surplus trousers and an ink-stained T-shirt, Dash focused his intelligent, dark eyes on Greg and waited for the editor to read his and Lauren's latest article.

Lauren leaned over Greg's desk, too. Meanwhile, activity in the campus newspaper office buzzed around them: keyboards clacked; phones rang; stacks of newspapers were carried back and forth; and reporters rushed over to the research area, back to advertising, and up to the editorial desk.

"Well?" Lauren asked.

"Come on, Greg," Dash pushed.

Greg was taking forever to read the story! Lauren was beginning to get nervous. It seemed like Greg was looking at the same page over and over.

"What do you think?" Lauren blurted.

Greg frowned. He thought for a moment. "I don't know. This is going to cause a major stink."

"Greg, we're not here to make nicey nice." Dash rubbed the two days' worth of dark stubble on his cheeks and readjusted the red bandanna that was tied around his forehead. With ink-stained fingers, he reached over and took Lauren's hand. "Every word of that article is true."

"Will you print it?" Lauren asked.

Greg looked up. "Can you two back up all your facts?"

"Of course we can back up our facts," snapped Dash. "What do you think we are, total beginners?"

Greg didn't dare accuse Dash of being anything but a seasoned professional, but Lauren was an inexperienced freshman. This would only be her third piece for the paper. Being a hard-nosed investigator was a whole new identity for her. Even though she'd given up cashmere and high heels for wire-rimmed glasses, parachute pants, and baggy sweaters, she wondered if Greg still took her for a chubby, pampered sorority misfit.

Sure enough, Greg glanced up at Lauren with a skeptical expression. He shook his head and looked over the article yet again.

Lauren turned her back to Greg and whispered to Dash. "Maybe we should have left out Mark Geisslinger's name." Although Lauren had been experiencing great courage lately, every so often her natural timidity came rushing back.

"Why?" Dash countered. "Mark did it. Mark Geisslinger and his Omega Delta Tau fraternity brothers made that freshman pledge get completely plastered and then locked him in a car trunk. Why should we leave his name out? We saw him with our own eyes."

"I know."

Dash looked down at Greg again and added, "Lauren, fraternity hazing is illegal. Before the university cracked down on hazing, fraternities pulled the worst pranks they could think of to test their new members. It got so bad that guys were even killed. It's a tradition that went out with the dinosaurs. At least it should have."

Lauren nodded.

"And if a few fraternity morons have decided that hazing is the cool thing to do again, it's our responsibility to expose it before it goes any further," Dash went on. "It's moronic to make some poor freshman do dangerous, disgusting things just so he can get into some fancy boys' club. And if we need to print every detail and every name in order for people to believe us, then that's what we'll do."

Greg cleared his throat and folded his hands. His cuffs were white and perfectly clean. Even his desk was orderly and neat. "Okay, Woodward and Bernstein. You can print any detail or name you want, as long as I'm sure it's all true."

"We were there, Greg," Lauren blurted, still clutching Dash's hand.

"If it hadn't been for Lauren," added Dash, "that poor pledge, Howard Benmann, might still be in that car trunk. Lauren was the one who saved him."

Lauren only allowed herself a little pride for her heroics, because remembering the way that poor pledge had been tortured and humiliated still made her sick. After getting a tip from KC,

Lauren had hid in the bushes and waited. She'd witnessed the ODT fraternity brothers pour alcohol down Howard Benmann's throat and lock him in the trunk of his own car. Lauren had finally screamed, scaring Mark Geisslinger and his frat brothers off, then pulled Howard out. By that time Howard had been black and blue, sick, dazed, and disoriented from his hazing ordeal.

"All right." Greg leaned forward. "But what about the Christopher Hammond accusation? Hammond is one of the biggest guns on fraternity row. If you tangle with him, you're really asking for trouble." Greg checked the article once more.

Lauren thought about Christopher. Christopher was more than a big gun. He was handsome, charming, a junior, successful in drama and track, and an intern at the local television station. He was also president of the ODT fraternity. Even though he hadn't participated in the actual incident, he had a lot to lose by being associated with anything so sleazy.

"You say Hammond didn't take part in the actual hazing incident," Greg made sure, "but he knew it was going to happen and didn't do anything to stop it?"

"That's right," Lauren asserted.

"And considering that Hammond is on the Interfraternity Council," Dash interrupted, "that's just as slimy as if he'd done it himself. The council is supposed to make sure that stunts like this don't take place."

"Which is why every word of this had better be airtight." Greg glared at Lauren. "Did you personally witness Hammond when he found out about the hazing?"

"No," Lauren mumbled. "Not personally."

Greg sighed.

Dash slammed his fist on the desktop. "We didn't need to witness it, Greg! We got confirmation on Hammond from a reliable, firsthand source."

"Who?"

Dash looked at Lauren. "A friend of Lauren's named KC Angeletti. KC overheard the frat guys tell Hammond about the hazing plans. Hammond told his frat brothers to leave him out of the messy parts, but to go ahead and do whatever they wanted. KC Angeletti told me that on the record."

Greg stared from Dash to Lauren and back again. He thought. He tapped his pen against the edge of the desk. He looked over the article one more time while Dash let go of Lauren's hand and slipped a tense arm around her shoulder.

"Well," Dash finally said in an impatient tone, "what's the verdict?"

"Yeah, Greg," Lauren prodded, feeling just as antsy. "Are you going to publish?"

"Or are we just going to pretend it never happened," Dash argued, "and let more guys rush fraternities and end up getting stuck in car trunks, or worse?"

Greg slowly pushed back his chair. He stood up and looked at Lauren and Dash. "Okay," he conceded, "you win. It's in the next issue. But I want it neat. I want all the facts backed up. And I want it finished and proofed by next Wednesday, before Thanksgiving vacation."

Before Lauren and Dash could react, Greg got up, gave them a weary smile, and walked away.

For a moment Lauren and Dash stood open-mouthed, unable to react. Then the next thing Lauren knew, she was in Dash's arms. He was twirling her around, as if he were a human merry-go-round. Lauren felt more than excited. Her cheeks were hot. She was dizzy, and not from the twirling.

Dash set her back on the floor. For a brief, wonderful moment he kept his arms around her. They looked into each other's eyes. They smiled.

Then, at the same time, they both let go, turned away from one another, and dove over

Greg's desk, where they started flipping through the pages of their story again.

"Do you think we need another paragraph here?" Dash asked.

"No. But I think we take too long to make our point about the Interfrat Council."

"Do you mean you think it moves too slowly? You tell me, Lauren, you're the creative writing major."

"It's not slow. But I'm not sure it's clear enough. Maybe we just need to rewrite the lead lines."

"Maybe we should just change the ending."

"Maybe we should. . . ."

By that evening, Lauren and Dash had gone over every word at least ten more times and were finally taking a break to celebrate their victory. They sat huddled together on the dock of the university's Mill Pond, watching the clouds float away, revealing a cold, late-fall sky. Water lapped the side of the pier. A clean breeze blew. Empty canoes chained to the dock rocked back and forth.

"Brrr," Lauren said, and shivered. She and Dash were the only ones there.

Dash slipped off his jacket, a satin warm-up parka with DODGERS written across it, and put it around her shoulders. "Maybe we should go somewhere warm." His voice was musical and quick.

"No. This is great," Lauren said. She liked the bracing air and the smell of the water and the grass. "Besides, I have to get back to the dorm; Faith, Winnie, and KC and I are all studying together for our Western Civ midterm."

"Ah yes," Dash teased. "Freshman requirements. I remember Western Civ."

"Stop bragging, Mr. Upperclassman. You have midterms, too."

"Just three or four. Or five or six." Dash stretched out on his stomach, rested his chin on his hands, and looked up at her. "I still feel like celebrating. I love it when I can nail a jerk like Christopher Hammond."

"How do you know he's a jerk?" Lauren wasn't sure what she thought of important, elegant Christopher. She'd once been fixed up on a prank date with him, and the result had been painful. Her own roommate, Faith, had just broken off a heavy romance with Christopher, but Lauren still wasn't convinced that he was such a terrible guy. "Do you know Christopher?"

"I don't have to know him," Dash tossed back with a touch of arrogance. "I've seen him in all those Inter-*rat* Council photos. I can tell. I've got a feel for this kind of thing. Believe it or not, I don't spend my entire life in a dark closet covered with newsprint."

Lauren laughed. "You just spend it at your desk, surrounded by year-old cups of coffee, stale sweet rolls, and a hundred crumpled up sheets of paper."

Dash took her hand. Her looked at her palm as if he were going to tell her fortune. "Which is exactly why we should go somewhere and celebrate by eating some real food. How about tomorrow night?"

Lauren thought for a moment and frowned. "I have to go to Tri Beta for one of my very last sorority dinners." She'd been invited into the prestigious Tri Beta sorority after her mother had forced her to participate in rush. But Lauren hated being a sorority pledge and couldn't wait to get out of it. "Thank God it's one of the last dinners I'll have to go to." Lauren raised her hands in mock prayer.

"A sorority dinner?" Dash frowned. "That doesn't sound like much of a celebration."

Lauren didn't need to celebrate. Lately her entire life felt like a huge, wonderful party. She'd started U of S as a stiff, terrified, out-of-place rich girl. The Tri Betas had only accepted her because of her mother and her wealth. For a while Lauren thought she would never fit in, but lately freshman year had turned around. She had three dorm friends in Faith, Winnie, and KC. She had her creative writing classes and her pride. Best of all, she had a sense of purpose. And, amazingly, she had Dash.

Dash let go of her hand. "So you really have to study tonight?"

"That is what people do in college. Especially right before midterms."

"I guess." He looked away. For a moment he didn't say anything. His dark eyes clouded over and his mouth tensed. "As long as you really do have to study tonight."

"Dash, I told you. Faith, KC, and Winnie and I formed a study group. We're going to meet in Winnie's room and study for Western Civ."

Dash drew a circle on her ankle. "Are you sure you don't really have to sneak off to some secret sorority voodoo session tonight, too?"

Lauren flinched. "What?"

Dash didn't look at her. "Are you sure you don't have to run back to your sorority house to leak the news of our article so they can do damage control before it comes out?"

For the first time that evening, Lauren felt the cold breeze all the way down to her bones. She shivered and knew that her usually pale face had gone even whiter. "Dash, that's really not funny."

"Why?"

"Because, I hate my sorority. One of the reasons I originally wanted to do this article was so that the Tri Betas would finally have a good reason to kick me out."

Dash sat up. He looked her straight in the eye with all the intensity of a muckraking reporter. "I guess I don't understand why you didn't quit your sorority as soon as we'd finished researching our hazing story."

Lauren didn't say anything.

"Lauren, sorority teas don't seem to go with the kind of stuff we've been doing. Why wait for the Tri Betas to kick you out?"

Lauren hadn't wanted to tell Dash the truth—that her mother had threatened to cut her off financially if she quit the Tri Betas. By forcing the sorority to kick her out instead, Lauren hoped to appease her mother. But she hadn't wanted to admit her strategy to Dash because it hardly seemed radical or brave.

"You don't understand sororities," she finally said, hoping to put an end to the subject. "That's just the way I have to do it. Don't worry. I'll be out of the Tri Betas very soon."

Dash moved closer. For a long time he looked

deep into her face with a serious expression. Lauren forced herself to look back with just as much confidence and strength.

"Don't you believe me?" she whispered.

He slid his arms around her neck. "I believe you. It's just hard for me to think that you go from me and the newspaper office to Sorority Row." He pulled back and kissed her lightly on the lips. "Oh well. I guess after our hazing article comes out, this topic of conversation will be a thing of the past anyway."

Lauren kissed him and then snuggled against his neck. "And it's about time," she whispered. "It's about time."

Three

ravis, what time is it?"

"Time isn't important, Winnie."

"Where are we?"

"In the world."

"Where are we going?"

"I don't know, beautiful. We'll find out when we get there."

Winnie and Travis had just raced under something that looked like a Chinese pagoda in the middle of a park somewhere in Springfield. Rain poured off tree branches and down the sides of the pagoda roof. Both Winnie's face and Travis's were covered with drops of water. Their clothes were soaked. A flash thunderstorm had come out of nowhere, drenching the mountains, the lawns, and streets. Lightning zigzagged across the sky.

Winnie stared at Travis's clean, all-American face. After meeting him at the bus station, he'd gone off to rent himself a room while she'd gone back to campus with Faith and KC to return the day-care van. Of course, she'd raced back downtown to see him again, even though she was due back at the dorms that night to study with KC, Faith, and Lauren. She couldn't be expected to ignore Travis after not seeing him for five whole months.

Still, Winnie worried about being late to meet her friends. She felt Travis's damp, slippery wrist to check the time on the sly, then remembered that he never wore a watch. Even when he'd left Paris, running to make a train to Spain, he'd guessed at the departure time, claiming that if he missed the train to Barcelona, he'd jump on one heading to Venice or Nice or Amsterdam instead. As long as he had his guitar, he'd said, he could sing on the streets anywhere.

"Travis, I have to get back soon," Winnie warned. "Faith and KC are expecting me at eight."

"How can you think about time when it seems like we just saw each other yesterday?" Travis asked, sliding his hands around Winnie's waist and lifting her onto a curved stone bench. "That should be proof that time doesn't really exist."

"I don't know. Maybe you're right." Winnie laughed and did a little waltz. When Travis leapt up on the bench and joined her, she giggled. "What does exist? Do we exist? Gee, I feel like something out of *The Sound of Music.*"

Travis bowed and held his arms out in a formal waltz position.

Winnie began to sing to the tune of "I Am Sixteen Going on Seventeen," in an off-key, silly voice.

> *I am eighteen,*
> *Going on nineteen.*
> *I'm a freshman at U of S.*
> *If I don't study*
> *For my Civ midterm,*
> *I will be in a mess.*

Travis bent her over in a corny tango move. He improvised a verse of his own.

> *I am nineteen,*
> *Not going on anything.*
> *Winnie's the girl I see.*
> *No looking backward.*

No looking forward.
That's the way I want to be.

Winnie laughed and tackled him. They both collapsed, sitting on the bench, then tumbled over onto the soft, wet ground.

"That was terrible," Winnie teased, even though the sound of Travis's voice had made her feel warm and woozy. "And you call yourself a songwriter?"

"Genius only strikes sometimes," he said, laughing. "So you have to be ready. And you have to take the bad with the good." He pretended to strum an imaginary guitar, then stood up and hopped around like a rock star, bending on a last dramatic note and scrunching up his face.

Winnie jumped up, applauded, then screamed and pretended to faint.

Travis caught her. The playfulness turned into something else. Rain dripped off his long hair and down her shoulder. Winnie felt her heart slamming away in her chest.

Travis kissed her, slowly, deeply, until the rain had turned to drizzle and the lightning had gone away.

"Travis," Winnie managed, trying to catch her breath. "I really do have to go."

"Right now?"

"Right now."

He stared at her, then leaned forward and planted a kiss on each of her eyelids. "You've got to do what you've got to do, beautiful." He took her hand and led her out onto the damp, spongy grass, running as he neared the border of the park.

"Where are you leading me?" Winnie called out.

"You ask too many questions," he said. Finally they reached a busy street.

Winnie realized that they were close to the center of downtown and had come out on McCarther Boulevard, one of Springfield's main drags.

"Do you really need to know all the things you ask about?" Travis asked, a little bit of accusation in his voice. "What time it is, where you are, where you're going. The Winnie I knew in Paris never bothered with all that useless information."

"The Winnie you knew in Paris didn't have to take midterms," Winnie explained feebly.

Travis frowned. He stuck his fingers in his mouth and blasted a whistle that could probably have been heard on the mountaintops. A rare Springfield taxi that had been heading down the other side of the street made an illegal U-turn and pulled up beside them.

"Where to?" grunted the driver.

"Travis," Winnie panicked, "I don't have enough money for a taxi." She checked the pockets of her man's suit jacket. "All I have is seventy-five cents."

Travis leaned in and asked the driver, "How much to take her to the U of S dorms?"

"Five bucks."

Travis handed the driver six.

"No, Travis," Winnie objected, "I can take the bus. You don't have any money either."

Travis opened the door. When Winnie got in, Travis leaned over and kissed her. "Money is like time," he said. "When you have it, spend it. Don't save it for a rainy day."

The driver was eager to take off, but Winnie refused to close the door. "But Travis!" She felt torn. Part of her wanted to jump back out of the taxi and spend the rest of her life hopping from here to there with Travis, never once worrying about what had come before or what was going to happen next. But another part of her could only think about the next week: Western Civ midterm on Thursday, French on Friday, History of Russia and Film Criticism at the beginning of the following week. In her mind she was ticking off how much material would be on each test, when she could cram, and what questions she would be asked to answer.

"Can we get going?" the cabby barked. "You want to make conversation, use a telephone, not my cab."

"When will I see you again?" Winnie asked.

Travis backed into the light rain. "When the moment's right. I need to check out the street-music scene and see if anybody's hiring for night gigs. We'll go our own ways for a bit, and then take it from there. Good-bye, beautiful!"

Winnie closed the door to the cab as the driver stomped on the gas pedal and sped away.

Winnie was only a few minutes late for the study group that was meeting in her room. As she walked down the hall, she passed Josh's open door. Her clothes were still damp and smeared with mud, and her hair wasn't just spiked, it looked Mix Mastered.

She stalled at the entrance to Josh's room. It sounded like he and his roommate, Mikoto, were having a study group, too. There were a couple of computer majors that Winnie had met when she'd gone with Josh to the Zero Bagel, a computer nerd hangout that served infamous goulash. And there were two other students that Winnie had never seen before. They all held books and notes and sat in a circle around a stash of doughnuts, sodas, gummy bears, and cheese.

No one seemed to notice her, so Winnie stood in the doorway for a few minutes and took in the scene.

"So doubling is a big theme, right?" asked Josh, who was clearly leading the discussion.

"Bipolar."

"Twins. Father and son."

"Rich and poor."

"Good and evil."

"Crazy and sane."

They all nodded. Finally Mikoto looked up and waved at Winnie. Everyone noticed her, including Josh. He flicked back his dark hair and offered half a smile. He was wearing a rugby shirt and old jeans. Even from the doorway Winnie could see his single blue earring and the woven bracelet on his wrist.

Josh noticed her muddy clothes and cocked his head. "Run through the rain?"

"Just get out of the shower?" joked Mikoto.

"Crawl into a drinking fountain?" hinted one of the computer majors.

"All of the above," Winnie answered. "What are you doing? Devising some new computer game?"

Josh shook his head. "All of us are in the same section of English Lit."

"Oh." Winnie stared at him. Even though he was holding back and still obviously angry, there was warmth in his handsome face.

"We'd better get back to this, Win," Josh said, looking away. "The test is tomorrow."

"I understand." Winnie thought about Travis and his vagueness about time. Josh wasn't fussy or meticulous. He was just down-to-earth. He had things he wanted to do and time he wanted to do them in.

"See you around, I guess," Winnie said, hesitating a moment longer in the doorway.

Josh didn't answer. His face was already back in his books.

Four

....

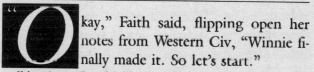

"**O**kay," Faith said, flipping open her notes from Western Civ, "Winnie finally made it. So let's start."

"Ancient Greeks," reminded Lauren.

KC waved her pencil. "Right."

"Who were they?"

"Dudes who wore togas and thought up our ridiculous system of sororities and fraternities," Winnie said as she flopped onto the floor.

Lauren tossed popcorn at her.

"Winnie, that's not going to get you an A on the midterm," KC reminded.

"Duh, Ralph." Winnie put her hand to her mouth in mock surprise.

"I'm serious, Win. You're late, too."

"Come on, KC. This afternoon I saw Travis for the first time in five months. I had to spend part of the day with him. And I just ran into Josh about four seconds ago. You try not thinking about those two guys all night and concentrating on the ancient Geeks."

"Winnie, I may be mellower than usual, but I still don't want to waste time," KC said. "I have my Intro to Business midterm tomorrow, and I still want to review that tonight, too."

"Okay." Winnie kicked her feet and recited in a robotic voice, "The ancient Greeks were people who shared the coastline of the Aegean Sea. They lived in city-states called poleis, or polis for singular. The poleis didn't share the same governments, or even the same dialects, but they worshiped the same gods, and the citizens called themselves Hellenes."

"Now *that* will get you an A on the midterm," Faith announced.

"Winnie, you make me sick," KC swore. "You'll do just what you did in high school. Goof off as much as you can, then cram at the last second and still get A's and B's."

"I hope so!" Winnie cheered. She twisted to look at her roommate upside down. "Hey, Melissa, what do you think?"

Winnie's roommate, Melissa McDormand, sat at her desk typing away on study notes for her chemistry class. "I'm sure you'll do fine, Winnie. If you study."

Winnie sat up and did a mock bow. "Thank you for your diagnosis, Doctor Melissa."

Melissa, who sat stiffly in her U of S tracksuit, smiled. She neatened her red ponytail and went back to her notes.

Meanwhile, Lauren salted the popcorn she'd brought. Faith passed out photocopies of her study outlines. KC opened her briefcase and supplied sharpened pencils and three-by-five cards. Winnie, however was a mass of disorganization, from her dirty clothes, which were draped about her room, to her notes and study guides, which were messily slung in pockets of fish netting she had tacked along her walls.

"Melissa, are you sure we're not disturbing you?" Faith checked.

Melissa continued to type. "No problem."

"Melissa has amazing powers of concentration," Winnie informed the others. "Unlike some people I know."

"When you're pre-med and running track at the same time, you'd better have amazing powers of concentration," stated Melissa. She checked her textbook and went back to her notes.

Faith gathered her Western Civ partners in a circle on the floor. It had been her idea to form the study group. After starting her production of *Alice in Wonderland,* Faith had begun to realize that she enjoyed organizing people and taking charge. "Okay, everybody. I know seeing Travis again was exciting. Lauren's newspaper article about fraternity hazing is exciting, too. Even my production of *Alice in Wonderland* is exciting. But let's get back to the ancient Greeks."

"Now *they* were a thrill a minute," Winnie cracked.

"Actually, they were pretty wild," Lauren said. She moved aside some of Winnie's incense sticks and cassette tapes, then squeezed in between KC and Faith. "Remember the lecture Hermann gave about the bacchanals?"

KC nodded.

"Okay, what else?" Faith asked. She pulled a highlighter pen from the pocket of her overalls and looked in her notebook. "What about the Oracle at Delphi?"

"It was a temple," KC said.

"Go on," Faith urged.

"Prophecies were made there," said Lauren.

Winnie interrupted, "I wish there was a place like that on campus so I could know the future, too. I'd find out what was going to happen between me and Travis. And me and Josh!"

"Winnie!"

"Sorry."

"Okay. Winnie, tell me about Pericles."

"Huh?" Winnie was staring into space. "He was a Greek."

"Winnie."

"Okay. Uh, he was king of Athens."

"No, he wasn't, Winnie," Lauren corrected. "There was no king of Athens. It was a democracy."

Winnie put her hands over her face and collapsed back against her bed. "Oh, no, you guys. I'm going to mess up again. I can feel it."

"You don't have to mess up, Win, if you can just keep it together like you have for the past month," said KC.

Winnie shook her head. "Look, I know this was a good idea to form a study group and all, and I will get it together for this test . . . eventually. But I'm sorry. I'm just not in the mood right now." She flopped over on her stomach, landing on top of her notes and some leftover cookie wrappers. "Maybe I should go outside and run a few thousand miles."

"Winnie," Faith sighed. "The midterm is in three more days."

"I know. I even told Travis I wouldn't see him too much until after midterms, so I could really study for all my exams. I wonder if I did that because I'm so flipped out over Josh and I'm not really ready to deal with Travis, or because I really do need to study. What would my mother the shrink say?"

"You need to study," answered KC.

"I know," Winnie moaned. "But look how well I'm studying."

Faith put her hand on Winnie's arm. "You just need to think, Winnie. You're probably smarter than any of us. You need to calm down, that's all."

Winnie nodded. She rested her head on Faith's shoulder. "You're right."

Faith knew she was right. She and KC had seen Winnie like this a hundred times before in high school. Still, Winnie had been getting it together, and Faith was surprised to see her revert to her manic state so quickly. Faith knew she was right in urging Winnie to use her brain and not get so crazy about guys.

Faith felt right about a lot of things. Ever since she'd realized that she was in a bad relationship and had broken up with Christopher Hammond, she'd felt as if a weight had been lifted. So far, her production of *Alice in Wonderland* had been going well. Her old friends and Lauren were getting along. Faith was finally feeling that her freshman year was on track.

She looked at her friends and closed her notebook. "I guess it's kind of late and a lot has happened today. Maybe we should stop for tonight and meet tomorrow after lunch."

"We could meet in our room and study instead of watching our soap opera tomorrow," suggested Lauren.

They all nodded. Even Melissa stopped typing and rested her face in her palms. For a moment they were all still as a door slammed in the hall and a stereo blasted in the Forest lobby downstairs.

After that Faith, Lauren, and KC waded through Winnie's junk to collected their notes and pens. They put on their sweaters. But no one seemed in a hurry to leave. KC lounged on Winnie's bed looking over her Intro to Business note cards, while Faith and Lauren lingered near the door. Even Melissa didn't resume her typing, but turned to sit backward in her chair and stare out the window.

"I'll be relieved when all these midterms are over," KC admitted, putting her cards down for a moment and shaking her head.

"Me, too," said Faith.

"Me, three," said Winnie.

"So will I," Melissa piped up.

Faith smiled at Melissa, surprised to hear her join the conversation.

"So what is everyone doing over Thanksgiving break?" KC brought up.

"Thinking about Travis and Josh and getting ulcers," Winnie blurted.

KC rolled her eyes. "No, you're not. You're going home, just like the rest of us."

Winnie nodded.

"Oh. I'm supposed to ask you all to Thanksgiving dinner at my parents' restaurant," KC remembered. "So now I've asked you. Will you come? You and your families? You too, Lauren. It's not that far. Jacksonville is just two hours from here."

"Thanks." Lauren smiled at KC. "But I might have to go to my uncle's house in San Francisco. I'll find out and let you know for sure."

"Okay."

"KC, was this Thanksgiving dinner your idea or your dad's?" Faith asked. She knew how embarrassed KC was by her hippie parents and their health-food bistro. Still, KC had changed recently. She'd softened and become more open. She no longer felt that her parents' laid-back lifestyle was at war with her conservative and ambition-driven personality.

KC shrugged. "It was my dad's idea. But I like it. I used to think I'd throw up if I had to look at another bean sprout or organic eggplant—"

"Yes?"

"What can I say?" KC laughed. "I'm giving my dad business advice now. I promised to help with the menu and introduce some new cost-efficiency measures."

All of them joined the laughter and soon they were all talking at the same time. They decided to take the gross midnight bus together to Jacksonville on the Wednesday night before Thanksgiving. And they refused to ride in Lauren's posh BMW, even if she did decide to come along.

The laughter and the chatter quickly quieted down again. Faith yawned. KC stuck her note cards in her blazer pocket and checked her watch. She, Lauren, and Faith started to head out the door.

Then Faith noticed Melissa staring out the window again. Melissa's face had paled under her freckles. Her brown eyes looked troubled, and she was chewing on her lower lip.

Faith didn't really know Melissa, but she respected how committed Melissa was to both athletics and pre-med. She knew that Melissa's family lived in the town of Springfield and that she tended to keep to herself. Faith was feeling so confident and on top of things that she followed through on an instinct to reach out to Melissa and include her in their group.

"We didn't mean to leave you out, Melissa," Faith said, quickly checking with KC. KC understood her questioning look and responded with a nod. "If you want to come with us to KC's parents' restaurant, too, you're certainly invited."

"Absolutely," KC seconded. "It'll be great."

Melissa momentarily lost her cool. She clutched the sides of her chair. She seemed to hold her breath. It took her a very long time to form an answer.

"Thank you," Melissa finally said in a tight, formal voice. "But I don't need to go to someone else's for Thanksgiving. My family has a great dinner, too. And, of course, I want to be with them."

"Oh. Of course," Faith repeated, not sure what she had said wrong. "I just wanted to make sure you knew you were invited."

Melissa offered a stiff smile. "Thank you."

After a moment of uncomfortable silence, Faith left with Lauren and KC, who were renewing the discussion of whether the Greeks had ever had a king.

* * *

Winnie stayed up that night to cram. She stuffed so many facts into her brain that afterward, she couldn't sleep. She mumbled. She tugged her sheets. She thought about Travis and Josh and the city-states of ancient Greece until she was punching her pillow and almost tumbling onto the floor.

At one-thirty she sat up in bed while across the room Melissa snoozed peacefully. Her insides felt like a kaleidoscope, where every time she turned she remembered something else that had happened between her and Travis. Every time she tossed, she remembered something wonderful that had gone on between her and Josh.

"I'll never be able to pass my midterms if I don't get some sleep," she muttered.

But her eyes were wide open. Her ears were picking up every sound. She tried putting the pillow over her head, but finally got up from her bed and put on her kimono and floppy bunny slippers. Making sure not to wake Melissa, she tiptoed across the room and out into the hall.

Forest Hall was considered a party-jock dorm, and there was usually music blasting, beer-can sculptures on the windowsills, and bulky bodies lounging in open doorways. That night, however, there was no one in sight. And only the low rum-

ble of the heater and the woosh of the wind outside could be heard.

Winnie tiptoed down the sterile beige hallway,
lingering in front of Josh's door. She wished that
when she'd seen him with his study group it could
have been more of a reunion. Instead, she'd felt
like an intruder, a mud-covered clown interrupt-
ing something that was important.

For a long time Winnie stared at that blank slab
of wood, as if she would eventually see through it
and peer into Josh's heart. She'd been keyed up
for her date with him the previous week. Winnie
knew that Josh assumed she had stood him up, or
that she was so late and flaky that she wasn't
worth dealing with at all. If only Travis hadn't
called just as she was leaving to meet Josh downtown.

Winnie lifted her fist and tapped, a soft knock
that hopefully wouldn't wake anyone else on the
floor.

No response.

She knocked a little louder.

Still nothing.

Knock. Knock. Knock.

Finally Winnie heard a rumble inside. She wondered if she'd woken Mikoto or Josh.

The person on the other side fumbled with the
doorknob until the door slowly opened.

"Hello?" Winnie whispered.

Josh squinted. He'd obviously been sound asleep. His eyes were half-shut, and his dark hair was matted to one side of his head. He wore a rumpled T-shirt, sweatpants with a tear at the knee, his woven bracelet, and one tiny earring. Winnie glanced past him and could see Mikoto stretched out, Josh's computer, and his desk, which was covered with books, papers, and floppy disks.

Josh recognized her, rubbed his face, and blinked.

"Did I wake you?"

"Yes, you woke me, Win. Of course you woke me," he said flatly, as if he were greeting a dorm prankster, not the girl whose door he'd once lovingly decorated with a computer-paper sculpture.

Winnie got a sinking feeling that this was just another screw-up and she was acting like a jerk again. Why couldn't she have waited until a decent hour to talk to Josh again?

"I'm sorry," she blurted. "I wanted to talk to you before, but there were so many people here and I know you were studying. Anyway, I just had to finally apologize for being late to our date last week. I got an important long-distance phone call from . . . an old friend . . . just as I was about to leave the dorm, and you know how I talk. After I finally hung up, I ran all the way downtown, but you'd just left. I think I missed you by ten minutes."

Josh looked at her through tired eyes that weren't adjusting to the harsh hall light. "Winnie, I have a midterm first thing tomorrow morning. I need to go back to sleep."

"I understand," Winnie said.

Josh waited one more moment. Then he reached out and took her hand. He squeezed it and offered a tired smile before closing his door again and leaving her in the empty hall.

Five

he next day, KC aced her Intro to Business midterm.

"All right, Angeletti!" she congratulated herself after leaving class and striding across campus. Her first important college exam was over. She'd studied. She'd been ready. She'd done well.

"Now if I can only catch up on my studying for Western Civ, English Lit, and Accounting," she sighed. "Maybe I can ace those exams, too. Oh please, Oracle of Freshman Grades, smile on me." She kept walking through the brisk sunshine, behind the campus bank, and onto the avenue that led down Sorority Row.

As KC waited for the traffic light to change, she glanced down at the big row houses and thought about how her life had changed. When she'd first arrived at the U of S, all she'd wanted was to be accepted by the Tri Beta sorority, as if that house's approval could give her the class and money she knew she lacked. But KC was beginning to realize now that class wasn't just a question of how important your parents were or how they lived, it was also a matter of how much you cared, what you accomplished, and what you stood for. Being a Tri Beta wasn't so important, after all.

Unfortunately, money was another story.

"I just wish I didn't have to worry about money during midterms," KC muttered as she approached the Tri Beta sorority house. She slowed briefly to notice the porch and the widow's walk and the Thanksgiving decorations in the front window. Each house on the row was more beautiful than the next. But of course, the Tri Beta house was the classiest of them all.

"Hello, Tri Beta house," KC muttered. "Bully for you."

She kept on walking. It amazed her that she didn't care that she hadn't been invited into that world, that for once, her own world seemed just fine . . . except for the nagging problem of money. Her father had given her a little extra on her recent visit home, but it hadn't gone further than a few typewriter ribbons, some extra books for English Lit, a poster for her room, and a new pair of shoes. KC was broke again, and she knew that her parents didn't have any more to spare.

The last thing KC wanted was to get into another bind like the time she'd overcharged on her credit card. The whole beginning of her freshman year had been tainted by that episode. She'd actually stolen money from the account for her soccer-shirt business project to cover her debt, and then had had to work on campus delivering the dorm mail in order to pay her business-class partners back. The only solution now, KC knew, was to find an off-campus part-time job.

After passing the Tri Beta house, the Kappa house, and Alpha Omega Delta, KC stopped at a bus stop bench, opened her briefcase, and took out that week's issue of the *Springfield Bee*. Folding the paper back, she checked the want ads again, concentrating on the ad for a salesgirl that she'd circled in highlight yellow. She checked the address of the store, which was called Mountain Supply, and went on her way again.

Mountain Supply turned out to be a sports boutique across the street from Luigi's Pizza. Stopping for a moment to check her hair in

Luigi's window, KC ran across the traffic, then paused to compose herself and coolly entered Mountain Supply. It was a small, colorful shop that sold mostly sports clothing, skis, and athletic shoes. Photos of white-water rafters dotted the walls, along with drawings of nearby snowy peaks and advertisements for ski lessons.

KC walked right up to the counter and waited for the attention of the man who looked like he was in charge. He was tan and muscular.

"Can I help you?" he asked.

"I'd like to apply for the part-time job you advertised in the paper," KC said in her most confident voice.

He looked her up and down. "Are you a runner?"

"I jog," she said simply. She wasn't about to admit that the only time she ran was when Winnie dragged her kicking and screaming to the track.

"How about rafting?" the man tossed back.

"Excuse me?"

"Which of the rivers around here have you rafted?"

"Well . . . none. But I plan to start rafting as soon as the weather turns hot again."

"What about mountain climbing?"

KC stalled. "I've always thought of mountain

climbing as an exciting sport. It's risky and beautiful and—"

He was beginning to look suspicious. "How about skiing? Do you know the runs at Mount Pendleton?"

"Mount Pendleton. Well . . ."

He sighed. "Look, my customers are mostly hard-core outdoor types. I'm afraid I need somebody who understands exactly what they need."

"Well, I may not be a great outdoorswoman," KC shot back, "but I am a great saleswoman, and I'm majoring in business. I'm sure I can learn everything about the sports and the different equipment. I just completed a very successful venture for my business class. We supplied soccer shirts to the dorm intramural teams. We ordered the shirts from Bernhard's Athletic Supply and turned a profit of—"

"That is impressive," the manager interrupted. "Unfortunately, I still can't use you in the store. I'm looking for somebody with heavy sports experience. Thanks for stopping in."

KC managed to stand tall. "Thank you for your time," she grumbled, wishing she hadn't used up valuable study time to answer the Mountain Supply ad.

She wandered back out onto the sidewalk and felt defeated. She had always been a pro at getting jobs in high school, knowing exactly how to look, what to say. She'd worked part-time selling perfume, cookware, toys, even modeling for the local department store. They'd never cared that she hadn't had any experience before she'd taken those positions. She only hoped that her new peace of mind wasn't destroying her business edge.

"Could that be?" KC asked herself.

She didn't know. All she knew was that she had a practical problem that had to be solved. If she didn't find a way to make some extra money soon, she was going to be in big trouble.

"This article is going to destroy me."

"Oh, come on, Christopher."

"You come on, Mark. You haven't read this thing. I'm on the Interfrat Council. My internship down at the TV station is really going well. I have a lot to lose right now. I can't afford something like this."

"Marielle," Mark asked, "what do you think?"

Marielle pointed a long, painted nail and waved it at the two frat brothers. "I haven't read the article either. But I've always said, if someone decides to go after you, you've got to go after them first."

At The Beanery, a coffeehouse a few blocks

from Sorority Row, Christopher Hammond was sipping cappuccino with his roommate, Mark Geisslinger, and Mark's latest girlfriend, Tri Beta sorority sister Marielle Danner. Mark was sprawled over two chairs, tugging on his dark mustache. Meanwhile, Marielle, wearing bright red lipstick and a chic navy suit, shook her chunky charm bracelet and drummed her long nails on the tabletop. Her hair fell in a perfect diagonal line across her face.

Christopher, in a crisp white shirt and tie, with his auburn hair newly cut, pulled out a Xeroxed copy of Lauren and Dash's hazing article. "Well, maybe you two should read this. Then you might not feel so smug."

Mark shrugged and took the pages. As he began to read, a Beanery waiter and waitress set up the small coffeehouse stage with a stool, music stand, and microphone. When they turned on the power, a scream of feedback echoed through the room.

Mark glanced up. "What's going on in here?"

"It's tryout time for new singers," Christopher answered. "We did a news story on it at the station a few weeks ago. They have open auditions and then hire new people for gigs at night."

"Oh, great," Mark griped. "I love being part of

amateur hour." He turned his attention to the article again, while Marielle swept her hair away from her face and read over his shoulder.

"Jeez," Mark breathed when he'd finished reading. "This is serious."

Marielle grabbed the article to finish it herself. Meanwhile, the first singer, a girl with short hair, tuned her guitar and launched into a song she'd written about saving the whales.

"Where did you get a copy of this, Chris!" Mark whispered, cringing as the girl hit a high note and held it as long as she could.

Christopher leaned over the table. "A guy I know at the newspaper leaked it to me. He thought I should see it so I could at least be prepared. It's going in the next issue."

"It's got our names in it," Mark said.

"I know."

"I could get kicked out of school for this."

Christopher nodded. "I could get kicked off the council and lose my internship."

"That wimp pledge, Howard Benmann." Mark flopped over the table and banged it with his fist, making his coffee cup totter and a piece of cookie fall onto the sawdust-covered floor. "We should have locked him in that trunk and left him there for the rest of his life. I should have known when he depledged the very next day that he was going to blab like this. I'll wring that worm's neck. I'll—"

Marielle scooped up the papers and interrupted. "Forget about Howard Benmann, Mark. He's just a useless twerp that you wanted out of your fraternity anyway. He's not the one we have to worry about."

"Oh yeah? So who is?"

"The people that wrote this!" Marielle pointed to Lauren and Dash Ramirez's bylines with her crimson nail. "Especially Lauren Turnbell-Smythe."

"Lauren Turnbell-Smythe," Christopher repeated in a foggy voice. "I know that name. Who is she?"

"Of course you know that name, Christopher," Marielle spat out. "Mark fixed you up on a date with Lauren as a prank during rush. She was your 'dream date'—ha ha—for the Trash Your Roommate Dance."

Mark scoffed. "How could you forget her, Chris? What a bowwow."

"She's kind of chubby, with mousy hair and expensive clothes."

Mark nodded.

"Now I remember," Christopher recalled.

"She's not so bad. She had nice eyes. And she helped me get a story once for the TV station."

Mark laughed. "Yeah, I remember her, too. From what I remember at that dream date dance, she hung around your neck like she'd died and gone to heaven."

"She did?" Christopher said, glancing up at the next singer with a confused expression. "Well, I don't know about that." He huffed and shook his head. "All I know is if we don't find a way to stop this article, I'm dead meat."

While the three of them thought, the Save the Whales singer was replaced by a fellow with long, blond hair wearing a T-shirt, an embroidered vest, black pants, and sandals. He sidled onto the stool, surrounded by two basses and an acoustic guitar. He set up the mike and began to croon.

"Oo," Marielle cooed, sitting up and staring at the blond singer. "Now this guy's pretty good."

"Are you thinking, Marielle," Mark barked, "or staring at the singer?"

"He's sexy," she said, purposefully grinning at the singer while Mark tensed with jealousy. The guy introduced himself as Travis Bennett, resident of Seattle and the world, then went on to pluck out another song.

"In case you've forgotten, Marielle," Mark

threatened, "we have more important things to think about. So stop drooling over some moron with a guitar."

"Cut it out, you two," Christopher snapped. "But Mark's right. We *do* have more important things to think about."

Marielle nudged Mark and gave him a smug smile. Then she leaned over the table again as Travis went on with his crooning. "All right. I'm telling you, this whole thing comes back to Lauren."

"Why?" asked Christopher.

"I just know, that's why." Marielle rolled her eyes. "I can't believe that Courtney, our illustrious Tri Beta president, ever wanted to let Lauren into our sorority," Marielle explained.

"Because Lauren's rich," Christopher said.

"I don't care how much money she has," Marielle argued. "The girl cannot dress, she's at least fifteen pounds overweight, and she's so shy she can barely get two words out without stepping all over herself. Loser city. But, of course, darling Courtney made me Lauren's big sister! Talk about humiliating."

"Wait a minute," Mark said, sitting up in his chair with sudden intensity in his wolfish eyes. "I don't know why I didn't put this together before. Remember I told you that after we put Benmann in his car trunk, when we were just about to drive back to the row, all of a sudden this girl popped out of the bushes and started screaming like she was in one of those *Friday the Thirteenth* movies?"

Marielle and Christopher nodded.

"I barely saw her before we started running," Mark recalled, "and it was dark and all, but I know now, that girl was bowwow Lauren."

Marielle narrowed her eyes. "So she didn't just write this thing . . ."

"She was waiting for us. She was there," Mark confirmed. "She set us up. And if she hadn't been there, none of this would have happened."

The three of them looked at one another.

"I'll tell you, I've wanted that girl out of my sorority from day one," Marielle swore.

Mark smiled.

Marielle picked up the article again. "I'm laying it on the line to Courtney. I don't care how sorry she feels for Lauren or how much she likes Lauren's mother's money. If Lauren Turnbell-Smythe isn't out of the Tri Betas by our next pledge meeting, our whole house is going to regret it."

"That's fine, Marielle," Christopher reminded. "But the first thing we have to do is cover our rear ends on this article."

"That's right, babe," Mark agreed. "We've got to stop this story from seeing the light of day."

"I know." Marielle looked them both straight in the eyes. "Just remember, the important person is Lauren. If it wasn't for her, neither of you would be in this nasty, stupid mess."

Six

innnnnniieeeeeee. Oh, Winnnn-niiieeeeeeee . . ."

Winnie was in the middle of the final essay question on her Western Civ midterm, but for a split second she thought she was in a dream. Or maybe it was more like a nightmare. Her mind had been focused so deeply on comparing the civilizations of the ancient world that hearing her voice crooned from the top of the lecture hall seemed like some surreal extension of Rome and Sparta and the city-states of ancient Greece.

"Winnnnniieeee!"

Heads turned.

"SHHHHHH!"

"Quiet!"

"Who *is* that?"

KC, Faith, and Lauren, who were sitting in Winnie's row, turned around to look, too.

"Winnnn!"

This time, Winnie knew it wasn't her imagination. People were craning their necks, shifting their feet, whispering, and scowling. KC had stopped writing in her blue book and looked frustrated. One of Professor Hermann's teaching assistants put down the papers she'd been grading, lifted her glasses, and glared.

"Winnie! Psssst."

"Oh, no. Travis!"

Travis was creeping down the aisle of the lecture hall as if he thought he could be inconspicuous with his long golden hair and his guitar slung over his back. He crouched over Winnie's chair, grinning like he'd just won a trip around the world.

"Win, I can't stand it any longer," he whispered, holding on to the side of her chair. "This is the time. I have to see you. I miss you like crazy, beautiful. And besides, I have to talk to you. I called your dorm and Melissa told me where your class was. I have incredible news."

"Travis," Winnie hissed, looking around and

fretting, "I can't talk right this second. We're taking a test!"

"Oh," Travis responded, standing up and looking around. "So?"

"So, you'll have to wait until I'm finished."

Travis looked disappointed. "Okay. Wow. Sorry, man. Should I wait outside?"

By now it seemed that more students were staring at Travis than down into their blue books. Most still looked testy, but a few of the girls had begun to smile.

"Yes, Travis, wait for me in the hall. I'll be done in a few minutes." Winnie looked desperately toward the front of the lecture hall. She nearly choked when she saw that the TA, who had stopped grading papers, was now storming her way over.

"Oh, no," Winnie sighed.

Travis knelt down next to her again.

"Travis, please."

"Okay, Win. I'll see you in a few minutes."

Winnie started to look back down at her exam, but Travis put a swift hand to her face, turned her toward him, moved in, and kissed her. It was a long, intense kiss, right on the mouth, right in the middle of her midterm! Winnie's head reeled.

Before Winnie could catch her breath, Travis finally scampered back up the aisle. Winnie stared down at her blue book. The exam questions no longer made sense. Her eyes went blurry and her handwriting looked like abstract modern art.

When Winnie looked up again, however, her vision became very clear. Joyce Weldon, the stern grad student who was one of Hermann's TAs, was standing over her.

"Ms. Gottlieb," Joyce said in a hushed, uptight tone. "Would you like to explain that little display?"

"I'm sorry," Winnie blurted. "He's an old friend."

"A 'friend'?" Joyce repeated.

"He didn't know we were taking a test. I didn't know he was going to come in here. I'm really sorry."

"I'm sure you are." Joyce picked up Winnie's exam and quickly looked it over. Then she glanced up the aisle after Travis and cracked a tiny smile. "You know, Ms. Gottlieb, I should confiscate your exam, but I don't think you were cheating. You can finish. Just don't pull a stunt like that ever again."

"Yes, Ms. Weldon. I mean, no, Ms. Weldon. I won't. Thank you."

Shaking her head but still smiling a little, Joyce Weldon walked back down to the front of the hall.

Winnie forced herself to go back to her essay, although it took her at least half the time left to remember what she'd been writing about. Out of the corner of her eye she saw Lauren finish her test, wave good-bye, and leave. Next Faith closed her blue book and gestured that she was running off to rehearsal. Winnie and KC didn't finish for another fifteen minutes. By then, they were practically the only two students left in the hall.

"That was a killer," KC whispered as they finally carried their blue books up the aisle.

"It was okay." Winnie tried not to look sheepish as she handed her test to Joyce Weldon, who took her blue book without a word. "Having Travis burst in at the last minute didn't help."

KC shrugged.

As soon as they were in the busy hall, any annoyance Winnie had felt at Travis disappeared. Travis had disappeared, too. The hall was full of people comparing notes on how their exam had gone, but not one of them had long blond hair, fabulous blue eyes, and a husky voice with a subtle southern drawl.

"Travis, where did you go?" Winnie moaned. Now that her first exam was behind her, she realized how thrilled she'd been to see Travis again and how heady his kiss had made her feel.

While Winnie fretted and searched, KC tucked

her briefcase under her arm and started down the hall. "See you later, Win," she called.

"Are you going back to the dorm to study for your other tests, KC?"

KC shook her head. "I wish. I'm going to go on another job interview. I hope I get this one. I'll have to study for my English Lit test later."

"I know how you feel," said Winnie. "I have French tomorrow morning. See you."

"Bye."

Winnie waved, then flapped her arms against her sides and looked around the hall again. She wondered if Travis had vanished from her life for yet another five months. Finally she turned and left the hall in the opposite direction from KC.

As soon as Winnie pushed through the double doors and marched out into the breezy fall air, she saw him. Travis was sitting on the ground in the plaza next to Plotzky Fountain. His back was against the concrete wall, his guitar was in his arms, and his handsome face was soaking up the fall sun. Winnie ran down the stairs.

"Travis!"

His eyes lit up like two flashbulbs as Winnie greeted him. Immediately he set down his guitar and was standing next to her, his arms around her waist. Winnie leaned into his chest and felt his long, soft hair brush against her neck.

He held her hard. "Man, I've missed you."

He didn't say anything about her exam. As Winnie held him, she forgot about her exam, too. She forgot about her French midterm the next morning and the History of Russia and film midterms she'd have right after the weekend. She forgot KC and Faith's warnings not to lose her head. For one short moment, she even forgot about Josh.

"Ready to go?" he said, picking her up by the waist and setting her on the fountain wall.

"Go where?"

"Exploring."

"Here? In Springfield?"

"Why not?"

"There's nothing to explore here, Travis."

"Don't say that, Win. There's always territory to explore."

Winnie's Parisian adventures with Travis came rushing back. They'd spent days exploring the city on what he'd jokingly called Travis's Tours. Sometimes Travis had read to her out of guidebooks. Other times he'd share tidbits of information on the famous people who had lived in the area or little-known events that had happened there. The best times were when Travis made up his own hilarious stories, improvising why the Eiffel Tower was shaped the way it is or the historical origin of the beret.

Travis held out his hand. "I don't know how long I'll be in town. We've lost three days already. I don't want to lose one second more."

Winnie flashed back briefly to her three remaining midterms. Travis had just said that he wouldn't be around for long, and she'd already waited three days to see him again. If she waited any longer it wouldn't be moderation and studiousness, it would just be stupidity. Maybe it was time to study Travis's way, in "the school of real life."

Winnie grabbed Travis's hand and ran out ahead of him. "Oh come on, Travis," she cried. "Let's go!"

It was nearly midnight. Winnie sat cradled in Travis's lap in a small park on the edge of downtown Springfield. Around them were some jungle gyms and benches and dozens of stray cats.

"The cats show up here every night. There's a guy who lives down that alley who comes out and feeds them."

"Incredible."

The whole afternoon and evening had been incredible. Travis had taken Winnie to the old Springfield train station and a greenhouse that grew orchids. They'd talked to people they didn't know in parks, on buses, and on the streets. They'd eaten lunch at an open-air market in the run-down northern district, sampling nuts and cinnamon rolls, beef jerky and spice tea. They'd walked and walked, and talked and talked.

"I just can't believe this town has so many amazing things in it, and all I know about is the university."

"I think that's why I decided not to go to college," Travis said. They both got up and began to stroll, hand in hand. "They make you think you're enlarging your world, but you're not. You don't find out about anything except what they tell you in the classroom. And as far as I'm concerned, there's a lot more to life than what's in books and on blackboards."

They walked alongside the railroad tracks on the east side of downtown, heading back in the direction of Travis's rented room.

"I know what you're saying, and I agree with you, sort of," Winnie said. "But you can learn things in a classroom, too. Right now I'm taking two history classes, Western Civ and History of Russia, and even though we're just finishing the ancients in Civ and we're only up to Catherine the Great in History of Russia, it all makes me feel like I understand the world I live in better. Does that make sense?"

"Maybe." They jumped over the tracks and went down Bybee Lane, a narrow side street of old boarding houses and inexpensive coffee shops. "Except you don't have to be in a classroom to learn all that. You could just read books on your own. I learned to write songs and to play the guitar through books and by listening to records. I never took a real lesson."

They stopped in front of the boarding house where Travis had rented a room. It was a dingy two-story clapboard house with a ROOMS FOR RENT sign out front and a harsh light shining down on the porch.

Slowly they walked up the stoop steps, lingering by the front door. Travis put his hands on Winnie's shoulders, than ran his palms slowly down her arms. He began to kiss her, lightly, on her forehead, her cheeks, her neck.

"Oh, Win," he whispered.

Winnie let everything swirl around her, allowing her real world to disappear again. The dingy porch, midterms, grades, and Josh were all forgotten as Travis's long, deep kisses made Winnie's whole body feel like it was floating. When they broke apart, Winnie was flooded with memories of Paris, memories of staying with Travis in his little hotel. Travis had been her first lover. Her only lover. When she thought back to that now, she wasn't sure why she had chosen him to be the first, or what that huge step in their relationship had meant.

Travis reached for the front door. "Come on up to my room," he whispered. "If we sneak past the front desk, they won't see you."

Winnie started for the door, but then something stopped her. It was the memory of how much she had hurt when Travis had left, and the thought that he would eventually leave Springfield, too. Now that the kisses had stopped, Winnie also remembered the pressure of her exams— and Josh. She hung back on the porch.

Travis gave her a confused look.

"It's really late," Winnie said. "I should get back to the dorms while the buses are still running. I have my French midterm tomorrow."

"So we'll speak French to each other," he replied.

Winnie looked away. "Travis, you don't speak French."

"So teach me." He took her hands and looked at her. "You either know the stuff or you don't, Win. If you ask me, college is for the birds. I don't know how you can take it all so seriously."

Winnie thought for a moment. Was she really

serious about college? She realized that she was. "I have to, Travis. College is my future."

Travis looked a little angry. "College isn't your future," he argued. "You don't know what your future is. Are you going to be one of those people who plans out their life when they're eighteen and dies of boredom at thirty? Where's the impulsive Winnie I knew in Europe?"

Winnie had to think. That person was still inside her, but she no longer wanted to give that part of herself free rein. "She's still here. I guess she just lives with another Winnie now, one that's a tiny bit more cautious."

"Caution is for old people, Win." Travis looked into her eyes for a long time. He made a move toward the rooming-house door.

Winnie held back.

Finally Travis sighed and pulled her in again. Winnie still resisted, so he let her go. "It's cool. Whatever you want, Win. I get it."

"You do?"

"Yeah. Come on." He took her hand and with a stiffer stride, led her back down the porch steps. "I'll walk you back to campus. I don't have any money for a cab this time."

"Okay."

They walked for a while, in silence this time, back over the railroad tracks, past shops that were closed and bars that were busy. There was almost no traffic and the moonlight covered everything. Winnie felt sad, as if she'd given up the opportunity to take a dangerous but thrilling leap into the unknown.

"Look Win, we should figure out what's going on here. Even though it's great to see you, I can tell that things aren't the same as they were in Paris," Travis finally said. They had reached the streets that surrounded the campus and took a detour through the fields used by the agricultural school, avoiding Fraternity and Sorority Row.

"It's just all these tests," Winnie explained, wanting to hold on to Travis a little longer. "I wish you hadn't come right in the middle of midterms."

"It's more than that, Win. Time passes. Things change. I didn't expect to be able to pick up where we left off. You know, I came to Springfield to see you, but I'm also just passing through, on my way to LA to see if I can break into the music business."

"Really?"

Travis nodded. "I know that you have a whole life here now and you can't drop it just because I suddenly show up. I don't think you want to, either."

Winnie wasn't sure what she wanted. She only hoped that everything would become clear soon.

Travis stopped under a streetlamp. He faced Winnie. For a while they stood there, looking into each other's eyes.

"Didn't you have something to tell me?" Winnie asked.

"Me?"

"Remember when you came into my class, you said something had happened and you had to tell me about it?"

"Man, where's my brain? This is what being with you does to me. I got a gig, Win."

"Where?"

"Right here in town. At a place called The Beanery."

"At The Beanery?"

"You know the place?"

"Of course," Winnie blurted. "It's a big college hangout. That's great. When do you start?"

"It's only one night actually. Next Wednesday. I went to an open mike audition and they hired me." Travis's happy face turned more serious. "Will you just do one thing for me?"

"What?"

"Will you at least come and hear me sing? My set at The Beanery starts at nine next Wednesday. Will you do that? Maybe we have a whole future ahead of us, and maybe this is it for you and me. I don't know. All I do know, Win, is that I want you to be there on Wednesday night to hear me sing. We'll figure the rest of it out then. In the moment."

"In the moment," Winnie agreed.

She was overcome with sadness as she realized that Travis was right, things between them weren't the same. She also realized that she was a little relieved to be let off the hook for the next few days, so she could study and figure out what was going on with Josh. But something else was tumbling around inside her. She was also thrilled that she would have one more chance to be with Travis and see if she could live life his way.

Winnie slipped her arms around Travis's back and kissed him. "Of course I'll be there to hear you sing, Travis. I wouldn't miss it for anything."

Seven

"**D**on't move. Nobody move. Everybody just take one deep breath, go back to your places for the top of the scene, and try it one more time!"

"But, Faith—"

"No ifs, ands, or buts. You almost had it. Don't take another second to think about it. Just go back to your places and start again!"

Faith crouched down to watch the repeat rehearsal of the scene in which Alice tumbles down the rabbit hole. Meanwhile, Merideth, her stage manager, sat next to her with a notebook in his hand.

"Go!" Merideth commanded.

The cast of seven freshmen and two children from the U of S day-care center began to move: backs arched and fingertips touched, forming a long, graceful tunnel, while Sara, the slender, pale nine-year-old who was playing Alice, threw herself into the mass of waving arms and legs, turning her body this way and that to give the impression of falling and falling and falling down.

"Add sound effects!" Faith directed.

An actor made churning sounds. Kimberly, the dancer who lived next door to Faith in Coleridge Dorm, wooshed like the sound of the wind. Jeremy, the other child from the campus day-care center, repeated "I'm late, I'm late," over and over again in a high, eerie voice.

"That's it!" Faith exclaimed, jumping up and clapping her hands. "Okay. Remember that. Remember where you were standing and how you got there. And keep the sound effects. They were perfect."

The cast collapsed on the floor and laughed. They began patting each other with open pride.

"That'll do it for today," Faith announced. "Thank you for your energy and concentration. I'll see you all tomorrow. Remember, next week we only have three days of rehearsal instead of five because of Thanksgiving break, so we'll have to work even harder."

A few of the freshmen moaned.

"I know. But we'll come back from vacation with even more energy." Faith smiled. "I'd like everyone to be off book as soon as possible."

"Pick up your trash," Merideth reminded everyone. "Jeremy and Sara, your moms are waiting for you in the hall."

Faith gathered her script and her notes and waited for Merideth and the cast to file out. After they were gone, she looked around the empty classroom in which they'd been rehearsing. She leaned her head back and grinned.

"Okay," she said to herself.

Faith didn't know where the final performance would take place, but she wasn't worried. She was directing the production to be experimental and sparse. The only costumes were leotards and pieces of colored fabric. There was no set. Hopefully, they would be able to do their final performance on a rooftop, in a park, or a bowling alley. This was an *Alice in Wonderland* of the imagination, and it could be performed anywhere.

"What a week." She smiled as she finally switched off the classroom lights and locked up. "And it's only Thursday." The hall was empty and quiet, and her cowboy boots echoed as she walked.

It had been a hard week, but a good one. Un-

like most freshman, Faith was finished with her
midterms. She'd only had two, and she'd taken
her exams in Spanish and Western Civ that week.
Stagecrafts class required practical projects but no
exams, and her other credits were coming from
her independent study production of *Alice in Wonderland.* Of course, every rehearsal of *Alice in Wonderland* was like a test, but Faith felt that she was
passing. Her creative juices were flowing. She and
the cast were having fun. She felt confident and in
control.

As Faith walked by the theater and Mill Pond
on the way back to her dorm, she remembered
how out of control she'd felt early in the semester. She thought about why her attitude had
changed so radically. She couldn't deny that her
family had had something to do with it. When
her parents and sister had come to visit, Faith had
seen that they weren't as perfect as she had always
made them out to be. That realization had jolted
Faith into facing her own life more realistically.
She'd ended her misguided romance with Christopher Hammond. And she'd renewed her friendship with her rock-solid old high school boyfriend, Brooks Baldwin.

"It'll be good to see Brooks again today," she
told herself as she reached the dorm green and
dodged a floating frisbee. She was on her way

back to Coleridge Hall, where she was meeting Lauren. From there, the two roommates were heading to the athletic fields on the other side of the dorm complexes, where they were going to watch Brooks and other dorm dwellers play for their intramural soccer league.

Faith trotted up the front steps of Coleridge, a coed dorm for students of the creative arts. As usual, scales were being practiced on a violin and a saxophone, the smell of paint and photo developer was in the air, and someone was tap-dancing in the lobby. Faith climbed the stairs to the girls' second floor, narrowly avoiding two dancers racing past her wearing layered leotards and jazz shoes.

Fiddling with her lock, Faith called through her room door. "Lauren! Sorry, I'm so late. Rehearsal was going so well that we stayed overtime. You and I had better hurry now though if we're going to see any of the soccer game. I hope it isn't over."

It wasn't until Faith had opened the door and thrown her script and books down on her bed that she realized that Lauren wasn't there. Instead, there was a note waiting on her desk.

> *Faith:*
> *Go on to the soccer game without me. I got*

called to a "special meeting" over at the Tri Betas. Courtney Conner sounded really weird when she phoned, so I have a feeling this is the big bye-bye Tri Betas. I sure hope so. See you tonight for the gory details.

L

PS. Tell KC I won't be able to bus it down to Jacksonville with you for Thanksgiving dinner next week. Sorry. My uncle left a message—I'm expected at his house in SF. I'm sure it'll be a snore.

PPS. I got an A on my descriptive piece for creative writing. Yay!

Faith quickly changed out of her overalls and into a denim skirt and cable knit sweater. For some reason she took a few extra minutes to rebraid her hair and dab on some lip gloss. Finally she ran out the door again and trotted back behind the new dorms, past the gyms, and over to the soccer fields, where a small crowd was gathered.

Right away, Faith spotted KC and climbed up in the bleachers to join her. She was surprised to see KC at the game since they hadn't planned to meet. But there KC sat, holding a textbook and looking stunning in a simple dark blazer and khaki slacks. Several guys on the next bench were staring at her.

Faith sat down next to her. "What are you doing here?"

KC looked up from her accounting book. "Oh, hi. I just thought I'd see how the soccer shirts are holding up."

"Well? What do you think?"

"They look good." KC chewed on the end of her pen. "Actually, I was hoping for inspiration for another business venture. I interviewed for two more jobs in town today. One was already filled and the other wanted someone who knows everything there is to know about car stereos. I gave my best sales pitch, but I guess they weren't impressed."

"Hmm."

"Yeah." KC sighed. "What are you doing here?"

"I'm done with my midterms."

"I hate you."

"Sorry. I wanted to watch the game."

KC gave her a funny look.

"I wanted to say hi to Brooks," Faith confessed. "It was so nice to see him again when I ran into him last week at the Soc Hop. I guess I wanted to keep things from getting weird again."

"Well, there he is," KC said, pointing her pen. Faith looked down at the field and saw Brooks directing his players for what would probably be the final play of the game. His blond curls were damp with sweat. His shoulders were broad under his soccer shirt. Even though he looked tired, he exuded his usual athletic grace and forthright sureness. Everything about him was straightforward and strong.

Faith put her chin in her hands and watched him. It felt so right to be on friendly terms with Brooks again. Faith had understood why Brooks had kept his distance from her lately. After being together for four years as supposedly the world's happiest, nicest, most well-adjusted couple, Faith had broken up with Brooks as soon as they'd both arrived at U of S. He'd been stunned and hurt and refused to speak to her for some time afterward. But Faith realized now that Brooks wasn't just her ex-boyfriend, he was a friend—period—someone with whom she had shared a huge portion of her life.

"YAAYYY! Yes. Let's hear it for Rapids Hall!" Faith jumped up and screamed as Brooks's team made a final goal and won the game.

KC smiled up at her and tugged her sweater. "You don't have to act like they just won the Super Bowl. They were ahead the entire game, you know."

Faith plopped back down and neatened her hair. "They still won, KC."

KC shook her head.

Faith waited while the two teams shook hands and gathered their gear. Brooks glanced up and spotted her, and for a moment she thought he would look right through her, like he'd done so many times since the breakup. But he didn't. He waved, trotted through the opening in the fence, and climbed the bleachers to say hello.

"How did you like the game?" he asked, smiling. He looked pleased with himself.

Faith was surprised to feel a hint of nervousness, as if he were someone she'd never met before. She was noticing how handsome he was and the way his blond curls framed his rugged face. "It was great. I just saw the very end of it though. My rehearsal went late."

"Oh, right," he came back easily. "KC told me you're doing some play as an independent study. You're directing it on your own?"

Faith nodded and smiled.

"Good for you."

Then neither of them said anything. Brooks kicked the bleacher and Faith sighed. It felt almost like old times. Well, old times with some weird awkwardness thrown in. Faith didn't let the awkwardness bother her. She didn't want to be in a romance with Brooks again. At least she didn't think she did. No. At that moment she didn't want to be in a romance with anyone. An awkward, renewed old friendship was good enough for her.

She sat there smiling at Brooks while he went over the plays of the game. KC rambled on about the midterms she had coming up and the plans for Thanksgiving dinner at her parents' restaurant back home.

Faith might not have said another word had she not suddenly recognized Winnie's roommate, Melissa McDormand, marching behind the bleachers, heading away from the track complex and in the direction of the dorms. She wore a stern expression, as if she were memorizing chemistry tables or hypnotizing herself into faster track times.

"Melissa, hi," Faith called down.

Brooks and KC halted their chitchat to look down, too.

Melissa froze, confused for a moment about where the voice had come from. She was wearing black spandex running tights and a U of S parka. Her red hair was tied back in a short ponytail, and her freckled cheeks were flushed.

"Oh, hi," Melissa finally answered, looking up and shielding her eyes.

"We were just watching the soccer game," Faith said. She scooted over and leaned on the rail. A moment later, Brooks joined her.

"Do you know Brooks Baldwin?" Faith asked Melissa. "He lives in Rapids Hall. He's captain of his dorm's soccer team."

"We won," said Brooks with a charming grin.

"Brooks, this is Melissa McDormand. She rooms with Winnie."

"Hi."

"Hi."

Then no one said anything at all. Faith realized that Brooks was staring down and Melissa was staring up as if neither of them had seen another human before. A strange, uncomfortable feeling started to bubble up inside Faith.

"Nice to meet you, Melissa," Brooks finally said, self-consciously wiping the sweat from his brow.

"You, too," Melissa said.

"Do you run track?"

Melissa looked down at her parka and nodded. Then she almost giggled. Faith was stunned. Whenever the two of them had been in Winnie's room, Melissa always seemed so serious, like a tough jock and study grind. Suddenly she appeared soft and girlish.

"I run the four forty. And maybe the eight

eighty, too, if I qualify. I'm in training now. We'll see what happens," Melissa said.

"I know how that is," responded Brooks.

"Are you going out for the regular soccer team?"

"No. This is just for fun," Brooks answered. "I'm in Honors College. I don't have time for the college teams."

Melissa smiled. She had a dazzling smile. "I know what you mean. I'm pre-med. I don't have time for the track team either, but I still do it. I have to, actually. I'm on an athletic scholarship."

They didn't say anything else, but kept staring at each other.

Faith abruptly turned away. She wasn't sure why, but she was suddenly very uncomfortable. "Come on, KC," she said. "Let's go back to the dorms."

Lauren had expected to face the whole sorority house that evening: the pledges, the active members, even the sponsors and the head of the alums. She'd pictured herself at the end of a long table, with all those refined women around her, shaking their pretty heads and saying, "Out, Lauren. Out. Depledge."

But it wasn't like that at all. It was only cool, blond Courtney Conner, the Tri Beta president, and Lauren's sorority "big sister," Marielle Danner.

The three of them sat in Courtney's room, an airy upstairs bedroom decorated with stuffed animals, ski posters, and lace pillows. Marielle lounged on the bed. Courtney paced from the dresser to the door. Lauren sat in Courtney's desk chair, like a prisoner about to be questioned.

"Lauren, is what Marielle said true?" Courtney grilled her. "Have you submitted an article to the newspaper that cruelly and falsely maligns our Greek system?"

Lauren wasn't sure where Marielle had gotten that angle. The only cruelty in her and Dash's hazing article was the description of what the Omega Delta Tau's had done to Howard Benmann. And not a word of what they had written was false. Still, Lauren didn't defend herself. She knew Courtney to be fair, even generous, and she didn't want to blow her big chance at getting kicked out. She merely hung her head.

"What did I tell you, Courtney?" Marielle whined.

Courtney gave Marielle a harsh look. Then she shook her beautiful head and knelt down next to Lauren. "I don't understand, Lauren. I've stood up for you ever since I first met you during rush. I know it hasn't been easy, but I honestly believed that you would eventually fit in here."

Lauren shrugged.

"Lauren, you didn't have to pledge," Courtney tried to reason. "You could have dropped out at any time. Why did you choose to do something so malicious?"

Courtney was starting to make Lauren feel a little guilty.

"I told you, Courtney," Marielle barked. "I told you she was bad news from the word go, but you wouldn't believe me. Maybe now you'll listen to my opinions for once."

Marielle's grating voice drove any guilt out of Lauren's head.

Courtney held up her hand to shut Marielle up. She took a deep breath. "Lauren, I'm sorry, but we can't have girls in our house who aren't loyal to the system. We just can't. I've thought a lot about how to handle this, and I decided that you should just depledge quietly, so we can avoid a big scene that will just embarrass all of us. Will you do that?"

Lauren nodded. "I will."

"I'm truly sorry that it worked out this way."

"Me, too," Lauren mumbled, meaning it for the split second that she looked into Courtney's classy brown eyes.

Lauren stood up and Courtney escorted her out of her bedroom. They walked down the stairs and through the living room, which was decorated for Thanksgiving with horns of plenty and gourds. Without a word they walked up to the door, where Courtney shook Lauren's hand.

"Good-bye, Lauren," Courtney said. "I always hate to lose a worthy girl, but I'm afraid you left me no choice. I do wish you the best of luck. I mean it."

Lauren knew that Courtney was telling the truth. "Thank you."

"Good-bye."

Lauren waited for the door to close behind her, then walked slowly down the front steps and past the other houses on the row. Once she was back on campus, she began to run through the cool night air. Any guilt she felt was quickly replaced by relief and unbelievable joy.

"It's over!" she cried.

Dash could no longer suspect her. No one at the newspaper could treat her like a spoiled brat. Her mother couldn't cut off her money because she hadn't quit but had been forced to depledge. Lauren was deliriously happy. She had never felt so free.

Eight

"Compare and contrast, compare and contrast," Winnie chattered to KC and Faith after her French midterm on Friday. They were in the student union, huddled around a plate of steaming french fries. "Compare and contrast ancient Greece and Rome. Compare and contrast present and past tense. I can't wait for next week. It'll be compare and contrast the developments of Moscow and Novgorod, compare and contrast the films *Citizen Kane* and *The Cabinet of Dr. Caligari.*"

"I still can't believe you get class credit for sitting around and watching movies," interrupted KC.

"Not movies, KC. Films. Actually, my film midterm will probably be harder than Western Civ. Our TA already warned us, it's going to be all essay questions."

"Hey KC," Faith said. "How was English Lit?"

"Ugh. There was one whole question on something we never even talked about in class." KC cringed. "It was harder than Western Civ."

Winnie squirted ketchup over her portion of the fries and dug in. KC, who was sipping a chocolate malt, tasted an occasional fry, while Faith ignored the fries and chomped on a fresh apple.

"I didn't think Western Civ was that hard," Faith said.

Winnie and KC exchanged glances, then chanted at the same time, "We know, Faith. And the rest of your midterms are over."

Faith took a big bite of apple and grinned.

"Compare and contrast, compare and contrast," Winnie repeated, shaking her head and making her long earrings swing. "After my French test was over, I kept thinking, compare and contrast Travis and Josh."

KC laughed.

"Okay. Travis is hot and Josh is cool. Travis is romantic and impulsive, and Josh is smart and thoughtful. Travis is a musician and Josh is a computer whiz. Travis thinks our relationship isn't the same anymore and is going to leave town and become a singing star. Josh thinks our relationship is toast and hates my guts." Winnie dropped her forehead on the edge of the table and moaned.

"Winnie."

"I must be the only freshman who's managed to ruin two great romances in the same year."

"Is it really ruined with Travis?" Faith asked.

"I don't know," Winnie sighed. "Maybe not. He says that things are different from the way things were in Europe, and I guess they are. But I have another chance on Wednesday night. My last chance to figure it out, I guess."

"What about Josh?" questioned KC.

"I don't know what's happening with Josh. Nothing may ever happen. All I know is that I'm going to study like a maniac this weekend, finish my midterms next week, go hear Travis sing at The Beanery on Wednesday, have a fabulous time with him, and run to the bus station by midnight to meet you guys and go back to Jacksonville for Thanksgiving—before I turn into a pumpkin." Winnie stopped for a breath. "Well, that's my future life in three words or less. What's new with you two?"

Faith started to say something, then reconsidered and bit into her apple again. "Nothing much. Just my play and looking forward to going home."

"My life is like this." KC held up her books. "Studying, tests, job hunting. Studying, tests, job hunting. I feel like a hamster in a cage. Maybe I'm getting too mellow, because I can't wait for vacation. All I want is to sit like a lump and eat my parents' cooking."

"Anything going on with Steven Garth?" Faith asked, referring to the guy KC had briefly dated from her business class.

"Nothing anymore." KC gobbled a few fries. "We see each other in class, say hello, and try to pretend that nothing ever happened between us. It's okay, though. I have enough on my mind right now without thinking about Steven Garth. I think I'm over him." She nudged Faith. "What about you? Have you heard from Christopher? Are you over him?"

"I think so. I haven't heard a word." Faith smiled. "I didn't think I would hear from him, though. I made it pretty clear that I didn't want to see him again." She looked down. "It's weird how suddenly a relationship can end. You're with someone and then poof! they're out of your life." Once more, she seemed about to say something else, something important, but Winnie interrupted her before she could begin to speak again.

"Oh, my God," Winnie squealed. "Speaking of old boyfriends, or rather, creeps I once went out with in a moment of weakness, there's Matthew Kallander, that guy I went out with over homecoming. He's in my film class." Winnie covered her face and whispered, "You sure couldn't compare and contrast Matthew. He's a definite multiple-choice. A, weirdo; B, fanatic; C, bore; D, all of the above."

Winnie shut up and plastered a smile on her face as Matthew waved and approached the table. He stood over them wearing a black turtleneck and black karate pants. His hair squiggled down his neck in a scrawny rat tail.

"Ladies," Matthew said, executing a little bow.

"Hi Matthew," Winnie chirped. "What'd you think of the study questions for the film midterm?"

Matthew cocked his head. He was staring at KC. "They were classic."

"I guess that means you'll do well." Winnie leaned toward Faith. "Matthew likes things that are classic: TV dinners, hot dogs, parades, *Leave It to Beaver* reruns. So what's up, Matthew?"

Matthew's eyes were still glued to KC. He was staring so blatantly that KC cleared her throat and shifted in her chair. Finally, Matthew grabbed a chair of his own and pulled it over to join them. He continued staring at KC as if she were a movie star or his long-lost sister.

"You are truly a classic beauty," he said.

KC bristled. "Excuse me?"

Matthew shifted to see KC's face from another angle. "Your face. The angles of your face. Those gray eyes and that dark curly hair. And those cheekbones. Those are classic cheekbones."

KC glanced at Winnie, as if to say, "Who is this guy kidding?"

Winnie shrugged.

Matthew reached in his pocket and pulled out a slip of paper. "My business card," he told KC.

KC picked up the card and read it out loud. *"Matthew Kallander's Classic Calendars."*

He smiled expectantly.

KC frowned. "So?"

Matthew flicked back his rat tail and moved closer. "So, I'm putting together a U of S calendar to sell in time for Christmas, with pictures of the most beautiful girls on campus. I'd like you to pose."

"What kind of pictures!" KC demanded.

Matthew held up his hands. "Don't worry. It's all very tasteful. It's classic. See, each girl will be made up as a movie star from the thirties or forties. Of course, one or two will pose in bathing suits. But if you don't want to, you don't have to.

With you, actually, I'd just like to get a close-up photo of your face. What a face it is."

KC sat back for a moment and Winnie felt like she could see the wheels in KC's head begin to turn. When KC sat up again, her recent mellowness had been replaced by a focused intensity. "You're getting this out for Christmas?"

Matthew nodded.

"Well, you'd better hurry," KC said. "You've still got to shoot the photos, print the thing, and distribute it!"

"I know," Matthew responded defensively. "We're shooting at the beginning of next week. Believe me, I know how late we are getting a start on this. That's why I need your answer right now. Will you pose?"

KC looked at Faith, then at Winnie, then at Matthew again. "I'll pose if you also hire me as your business consultant, which means you cut me in on twenty percent of the profits."

"But . . ."

"That's a deal breaker," KC argued desperately. "No business cut, no posing. Don't worry, I'm worth it. My advice will increase your profit by at least twenty percent."

Matthew's blue eyes suddenly seemed to be swimming in his face. "Um, well, okay. It's a deal."

KC shook his hand. "Oh. One more thing, Matthew."

"Huh?"

"Having a calendar with only girls pictures in it is sexist. Why not have half the pictures be of great-looking guys?"

Matthew thought for a moment, then grinned. "Yeah. I like that idea. That's classic!"

"You bet it is," said KC.

That night was a classic in Winnie's dorm—classically raucous. No one seemed to care that they were in the middle of midterms. To Forest residents, it was an ordinary Friday night, with stereos turned up so high that windows trembled and floors shook.

"MELISSA," Winnie yelled at her roommate, who was sitting at her desk with her back to Winnie.

Melissa didn't even turn around. She managed to study by wearing a Walkman on which she played vocabulary tapes she'd made for her German class.

Winnie walked over and plucked off Melissa's earphones. Melissa looked around, momentarily confused, as if she'd just been woken out of a dream. "Yes?"

"I'm going to the study room downstairs."

Winnie realized that she was still practically yelling and lowered her voice. "Do you want me to bring you anything from the machines when I come back? A cup of coffee or a candy bar or anything?"

Melissa held up a half-eaten protein bar and shook her head. "No thanks."

"Okay. See you later." Winnie picked up her notes and her History of Russia book and left the room.

"Oh, great," Winnie grumbled as soon as she was out her door. Just getting downstairs was going to be a trial. At one end of the hall, some basketball guys were throwing water balloons, and at the other end two football players were dragging a third guy out of the bathroom and swinging him by his hands and feet.

"Coed dorms," Winnie grumbled as she snuck past the male jock rowdiness. Trotting downstairs, she wondered whatever could have made her want to live in a dorm where girls and guys roomed on the same floor. At least in Faith's dorm, the floors were divided by sex. Maybe KC, in her girls-only study dorm, had the right idea.

The Forest Hall study room was a soundproof cubicle in the basement, around the corner from the laundry room and snack machines. After a quick detour to buy a Coke, some peanuts, and a bag of corn chips, Winnie tucked her textbook and notes under her arm and pushed open the door.

There was already someone inside, bent over the rectangular table. His books were spread over the whole tabletop and dark hair hid half his face. Winnie saw the woven bracelet around his wrist and the the curve of his slim back and she knew it was Josh.

Winnie considered making a quick exit, but Josh looked up first. He stared at her and didn't say a word, then cleared his books from half the tabletop. He went back to his work, while Winnie put down her textbook and her notes and sat across from him.

Winnie tried to read. She tried to memorize dates and places. She even tried to eat corn chips without making any noise. But soon, she couldn't stand it any longer. The facts of medieval Russia weren't sticking in her head, while the corn chips were sticking to the roof of her mouth.

Finally she took the stack of Post-its that she used to mark important pages in her textbook and peeled off the top sheet. She scribbled, *"Hi, I'm Winnie. Remember me?"* on the little pink square and stuck it on the back of Josh's hand.

Josh stopped writing. He peeled off the Post-it and read it. Then he scribbled something else on it and, without looking up at Winnie, managed to stick it right on her chin.

Winnie plucked the note off her face and read it. *"I remember,"* it said. *"How could I forget. Besides, I'm not the forgetful one."*

Winnie peeled off another little sheet. *"I'm sorry I messed up on our date. It was an honest mistake. I'm honestly sorry. Honestly. I'm sorry I woke you up the other night, too."*

Josh wrote back, *"Everyone makes mistakes."*

That gave Winnie hope and she couldn't keep her mouth shut any longer. Someone had to take the initiative, and she decided that she would be the one. "Josh," she blurted, "can't we get together and talk out loud? Can't we clear this mess up, just get together face-to-face for an hour or so, sometime before we leave for vacation?"

Josh just looked at her.

Winnie babbled on, "My mother, she's a psychologist, and she says that you have to talk about things, get things out in the open and all that. She meets people for an hour at a time to talk about their problems, so maybe we should just meet for an hour and talk about . . . us."

When Winnie finally stopped talking, one side of Josh's mouth lifted in a tiny smile. He took one of her chips and munched on it. "I don't know, Win. An hour's kind of a big chunk of time. I still have to study for three midterms. One test is on Monday and two are on Wednesday. And then Thursday's Thanksgiving."

"So what about Wednesday night?" Winnie blurted, unable to stop her mouth. "After you finish your exams but before we all go away for vacation. Can't we get together and talk then? Just for a little while. Just to touch base before we go away for four days and things get even weirder."

Josh gathered his papers with a pensive expression. He got up and took a step toward the door, as if he were going to leave without answering. Then at the last minute he turned back, bent over, and kissed her on the top of the head. "I'd like that, too. Let's make it ten-thirty Wednesday night," he said. "There's a computer-major party at someone's house off campus, but I should be back by then. Let's meet in the dorm lobby."

"Okay! Let's meet then."

Josh nodded and slipped out the door.

"YES!" Winnie cheered, realizing how much a second chance with Josh meant to her. "YES!"

It was only after Winnie had danced and sung and jumped up and down with joy that she remembered that Wednesday was the also the night she was going to The Beanery to meet Travis.

Nine

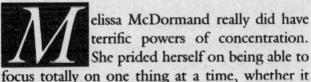**M**elissa McDormand really did have terrific powers of concentration. She prided herself on being able to focus totally on one thing at a time, whether it was chemistry, biology, German, English composition, or track. She also worked harder than most people.

Even on Sunday, she was pushing herself to the limit. She was in the university gym's weight room, concentrating on a bench press. She focused her mind on the grip of her hands, her rhythmic breathing, the straightness of her back, and the relaxation of her neck. She was so concentrated that when she sat up after her third set, she was stunned to see Brooks Baldwin sitting on the next bench, smiling at her. He was in his soccer clothes and a few blond curls were plastered to his forehead. He had that same serene, trustworthy expression she remembered from when she'd met him after the soccer game. She wondered how long he'd been watching her.

"Do you want me to spot you for your next set?" he asked.

Melissa was surprised to find her concentration broken. "What?"

He got up and stood over her barbell. "I'll spot you if you want to try another set. Do you want to increase your weight?"

Melissa was already lifting at her limit. "Sure. Add ten more pounds."

Brooks secured an additional five-pound plate on either side of the barbell.

Melissa took a deep breath and lay back on the bench. As she grabbed the bar, she looked up at Brooks's handsome face. She checked the position of her shoulders and elbows, then began to lift.

"Come on," he encouraged as she pressed the weights up and down. When she started to tire, he urged, "One more. You can do one more. Come on."

Melissa strained her way through a few more repetitions.

"One more!"

"That *was* one more," she groaned.

"So do one more after that. One more!"

Melissa kept lifting until her arms began to tremble and she could no longer press the barbell off her chest. Sweat zipped down the side of her neck.

Finally, Brooks took the weight from her and put it back on the rack.

Melissa shook out her arms and sat up. "That was great. Thanks."

"You're tough," he said with appreciation.

"It's all in the mind."

He smiled. "You have a tough mind, then."

"You can say that again."

They laughed. Melissa felt a tiny crack being carved in the veneer of toughness she always kept up.

"Do you work out with weights a lot?" Brooks asked.

Melissa slid onto the floor and began doing stretches. "A couple times a week. My coach thinks it will improve my running times."

Brooks nodded. He picked up a dumbbell and sat on a workout bench, doing tiny wrist curls with perfect form.

"You've worked out with weights, too, I see."

He smiled. "I fooled around with them a little

in high school, for the same reason as you. My coach thought it might help me with soccer."

"Did it help?"

"Yeah. Whenever you work hard at something, it usually pays off."

"I agree."

Then it happened again, that strange staring that had happened the other day when Melissa had met Brooks after his soccer game. It felt as if their eyes were suddenly glued together, as if looking away would be almost impossible. Melissa realized that she liked the way Brooks looked, his blond curls, athletic body, and bright, straightforward eyes. He seemed together and strong. Even the fact that he was associated with Winnie's old friends appealed to her. She liked Winnie, KC, and Faith. Sure, Winnie was kind of flaky, but as a trio they seemed together and strong, too.

"So, are you here to work out?" she managed, looking away and breaking the connection between them.

He shook his head. "I was just at soccer practice. I was walking back to the locker room, and I saw you. So I came in to say hello."

Their eyes reconnected, and this time it was too much for Melissa. "You came in to make sure I wasn't wimping out on my lifting."

"No." He stared straight at her. "Actually, I

came in to see if you might want to go out with me sometime."

His directness suddenly made Melissa feel defensive. She was attracted to him, but she hadn't been prepared for that next step. She grabbed a towel and headed for the squat rack. "I'm too busy to date. Thanks, but between classes and track, I don't really have time."

"Oh." He didn't follow her. Instead he offered a confused smile and backed toward the door. "Okay. I'm busy, too. So, I guess maybe I'll see you around the dorms."

"Yeah. I guess so. See you." Melissa watched Brooks go, staring after him long after he had disappeared down the hall.

"Bye," she whispered.

Melissa liked Brooks, but she didn't want things to go any further. As far as she knew, getting close to people only meant pain. And she had already had enough of that to last her a lifetime.

Lauren didn't call her parents every Sunday.

Unlike Faith and so many other freshmen in Coleridge Hall, she didn't phone home to tell her mother about every pancake breakfast, every assignment, and every new friend. She didn't have to know what was going on in the old neighbor-hood and what the gossip was from home.

Lauren didn't really feel that she had a home. Her parents had a house outside New York City, but they were rarely there. Most of the time they were traveling in Europe, the Orient, or the Middle East. As far as she was concerned, family and home were things she read about in short stories and plays.

"I'd like to charge this call to my credit card, please," Lauren told the operator. She was using the pay phone in the foyer outside the dining commons. Students walked by and there was the distant clanging of dishes being washed in the kitchen. Sunday dinner had just been served.

"You know, miss, you can save money if you dial that overseas number directly," the operator told her.

"That's okay," Lauren said. That was another thing Lauren didn't share with the other creative-arts majors in her dorm. She didn't make up elaborate calling codes so that her parents could call her back when the rates were cheap. She never worried about what things cost or how she would pay for them.

"The Turnbell-Smythes are in suite six hundred," a woman with a British accent said after the operator had put Lauren through. Lauren's parents were in London that weekend, staying at an exclusive Kensington Garden hotel.

"Hold on, please."

"Thank you." Lauren waited as the phone rang and rang. On the seventh ring, someone finally picked up. "Mother?"

"Who is this?" Lauren's mother sounded sleepy and confused.

"It's me, Mother. Lauren."

"Lauren, do you know what time it is!"

"It's six o'clock."

"Lauren, it may be six o'clock at that godforsaken school of yours. But here, it's one in the morning."

"Oh. I'm sorry." Lauren wished she'd remembered about the time difference and caught her mother in a better mood. Still, nothing could ruin the pleasure she would have delivering her victorious news.

"What's wrong?"

"Nothing's wrong, Mother. I just called to talk."

Her mother huffed loudly. "Fine. Talk. I'm awake now. Talk."

Lauren closed her eyes and took a deep breath. She thought about Dash and the newspaper. She thought about Marielle, Christopher Hammond, and sleazy Mark Geisslinger and began to smile.

"I wanted you to know what's been happening with the Tri Betas."

"Oh?" Her mother's voice finally livened. "You're starting to like it better, aren't you? I told you that if you gave it a chance, the sorority would turn that cowboys-and-Indians school of yours into something worthwhile."

"Well, actually Mother, that isn't quite the way it's ended up."

"What does that mean?"

"Mother, I gave the Tri Betas a chance. I really did. But now they don't want to give me one. Um, they asked me to leave the sorority."

"What?"

"I tried, Mother, I really tried. But it just didn't work out. It's not my fault."

"I'll call someone from the council," her mother barked. "I'll get you back in, Lauren. Don't tell me it just didn't work out. We'll make it work out."

"Mother, you can't do that. I tried to fit in with the Tri Betas and they didn't want me. Let's leave it at that!"

There was a pause while the overseas line crackled. "Lauren, don't give me this," her mother finally said. "I wasn't born yesterday. Don't forget that I was a Tri Beta, and I know how sororities work."

"I know."

"They don't force a pledge, especially a girl with your resources, to depledge unless that girl really asks for it."

"Mother, what is that supposed to mean?"

"You know very well what it means."

Lauren held her breath.

"That's it, Lauren. I've had enough of your idiotic behavior. You refused to go to a private college in the East. You wanted to go to some godforsaken state school in the West, and I let you go—on one condition: that you join that sorority. Well, you've let me down, and as far as I'm concerned our agreement is off."

"Mother, they asked me to leave. I didn't quit!"

"I don't care how it happened. If you insist on staying at that school, you'll pay for it on your own. And don't say I didn't warn you. You are not getting one penny from your father or from me. Not until you come to your senses and move back home."

"Mother!"

"There's nothing more to be said. When you're ready to apologize and move back east to start a decent private school, you let me know. And when you do decide, please call at a reasonable hour."

Lauren's mother hung up.

"Thanks a lot, Mom," Lauren muttered. For a few minutes, she stood in the phone booth letting her heart slow down and her mind clear. She almost cried, until her newfound courage pushed back the tears and gave her hope.

Lauren strode back to her dorm. As she rushed up the stairs she took great pleasure from the sound of a jazz combo and Freya, her neighbor, singing an aria next door. She loved looking at the murals and the photographs, the pieces of half-finished sculpture and the notices about writers' groups.

"This is where I belong," Lauren swore, "and I'm not leaving."

Ten

"KC, don't move. Not unless you want to end up looking like something out of *Cats*."

KC squirmed.

"KC."

"I can't help it, Faith. It's weird having someone else put makeup on your face. I keep feeling like I'm going to twitch."

"You won't twitch."

"Where did you learn how to do this, anyway? You almost never wear makeup."

"I'm a drama major, KC. We study this kind of thing. Besides, this make up is for photography. That's different than everyday makeup."

It was Tuesday, and KC was getting ready for her photo shoot. She'd finally made it through her midterms, although she'd ended up spending more time over the weekend arranging and planning Matthew's classic calendar than she had studying for her accounting test. She'd had to. Since she hadn't found a part-time job, she'd decided that the calendar was going to pay for dinners out and extra books.

"I hope this makeup isn't too different from everyday." Worried, KC leaned to check her face in the hand mirror. "I have a business interest in Matthew's calendar now. It won't sell if there's a freshman in it who looks like The Joker."

"Have confidence, KC. You could never look like The Joker. When I'm through with you, you'll look like Katharine Hepburn."

"Are you sure this lipstick isn't too heavy?"

"I'm sure," Faith assured her. "The lights and the camera make three-quarters of it disappear."

"Okay. You know, I don't want to look like Bozo the Clown, either."

"You won't."

"I don't want anything in this calendar to look Bozoish."

KC and Faith were in the study cubicle in the basement of Coleridge Hall. KC had arranged for them to shoot the calendar photos in the creative-arts dorm's basement, as opposed to Matthew's idea of paying two hundred dollars to rent a studio downtown. KC had even convinced Matthew to use Peter Dvorksy, a talented Coleridge resident, as the calendar's photographer. KC had also convinced Faith to take a few hours away from rehearsing *Alice in Wonderland* to help with makeup and clothes.

"How's Peter doing?" KC asked, lurching to the side again.

"Fine," Faith stated, grabbing KC's shoulders and holding her still. "It's a good thing he's a guy. I couldn't concentrate if I were shooting that gorgeous Warren."

"Tell me about it."

"When I had to make Warren up as Clark Gable, I thought I'd drool on his tuxedo."

KC laughed. "Even I, who am not a drooler, know what you mean. Peter found him. He's a senior. I guess he modeled for other photography students. He is gorgeous, isn't he? I think my idea of including guys was a good one."

"Not bad." Faith threw up her hands. "KC, if you move one more time, I'm going to give you a black eye, and I'm not sure if it will be makeup or the real thing."

"Okay."

Faith began shading KC's cheeks with a soft

brush, making her high cheekbones look even more pronounced. "So we're all set for the bus ride home tomorrow night?"

KC nodded. "Vacation. At last."

"Do we have to wait for the midnight bus? My rehearsal is over at five."

KC leaned toward the mirror and blotted her lipstick. "The midnight bus is the only one that doesn't stop in every cow town along the way and take five times as long. I just hope Winnie isn't a basket case the whole way home. I still can't believe she made dates with Travis and Josh for the same night. Only Winnie could do something like that."

Faith teased KC's curls. "Winnie was born for hard-to-handle situations. I guess she's arranged to hear Travis sing at The Beanery and then plans to race back to campus to have her chat with Josh. At least she thought about the possibility of being late this time. Lauren's going to let Winnie use her BMW, so for once, Winnie may be on time and pull it off."

"That was nice of Lauren to let Winnie use her Beamer," KC commented. She stood up and stepped into high heels. "Lauren has been getting more and more generous lately."

"Generous isn't the word," said Faith as she knelt down and checked KC's hem. "Ever since yesterday, when she told her mom about getting kicked out of the Tri Betas, Lauren has been practically giving all her stuff away."

"Really?"

Faith nodded. "She gave three cashmere sweaters to Freya, the opera singer from Germany who lives next door to us. Then she gave Kimberly her CD player and donated her microwave and TV to the floor common room."

"Well, people change." KC laughed and looked at herself in the full-length mirror they had brought over from the costume shop. "Look at me. I'm not so embarrassed by my parents now, and I'm actually excited about going home. And I've just changed from Kahia Cayanne Angeletti, U of S freshman, into Katharine Hepburn."

In the middle of KC and Faith's laughter, there was a knock on the cubicle door.

"Come in. We're all decent," Faith called.

The door swept opened and Matthew Kallander entered. He was wearing all black again, with a string tie studded with pieces of turquoise. A camera lens hung from a cord around his neck, and he kept holding it up to look at KC through it. In his other hand, he held a clipboard.

"Classic," Matthew said, and nodded. "I love the suit and the hair."

KC smiled. She was wearing a forties suit that

Faith had borrowed from costume storage. It had shoulder pads and a tight, straight skirt. Her hair was tightly curled and pulled back on either side with combs. Faith had also given her thin, arching eyebrows and a determined, red mouth. "Thanks, Matthew."

Matthew leaned against the wall and looked over his clipboard. "Peter will be finished shooting Warren in a few minutes, and then it's your turn, KC. In the meantime, let's go over the schedule we talked about. Okay?"

KC nodded.

"Peter says he can get proofs of the photos right away."

"Good," KC replied. "What we have to do then is put together a mock-up calendar, a quick, make-shift version that we can take around to whomever runs the Christmas craft fair on campus and the student store, so they can see what we're doing and hopefully agree to stock it. We're incredibly late to get something on the market for Christmas, so we've really got to rush."

Matthew nodded and took notes. "I'll make the mock-up of the calendar while you're home for Thanksgiving break."

"You're not going home, Matthew?" Faith asked.

Matthew shook his head. "I want to stay here

by myself. I like a few days alone every once in a while so I can watch old movies and eat classic things like Spam and dips and potato chips with ridges in them."

KC and Faith exchanged glances.

Matthew stared at KC again. "Okay. Well, I'd better start making calls and find out who runs the student store."

"Good idea, Matthew."

Matthew looked at KC through his lens once more and then swept out.

"Matthew's an original, isn't he?" said Faith.

KC laughed. "You could say that. Oh well, at least he isn't one of the two guys Winnie is going nuts over. We have to give her credit for that."

Faith nodded, then turned as there was another knock on the door. This knock was much softer and more polite.

"It's open," Faith called. "Come in."

The door opened slowly. Standing in the doorway was a girl with her ash blond hair in curlers, carrying a makeup case and a dress in a plastic bag. Even though she wasn't wearing a spot of makeup, her beauty was undeniable. It was Courtney Conner, president of the Tri Betas, who had taken KC under her wing during rush. Since KC's lack of sorority success during her first week at U of S, she had barely been able to look Courtney in the eye.

"Courtney, come in," KC said in a more formal, slightly nervous voice. "I'm so glad you agreed to take part in this."

Courtney smiled and set down her things. "I thought it might be good publicity for the Tri Betas."

"It will be," said KC.

"Hi Courtney. I'm Faith. I'll be helping to make you look like Grace Kelly."

"I brought some things, too," Courtney said.

"Good," said Faith. "Have a seat and we can get started."

KC stared at Courtney until Peter could be heard calling for her to come out and pose. "I have to go," KC said.

Courtney sat perfectly still as Faith put on her makeup.

KC stopped in the doorway and turned back. "Thanks for coming, Courtney. I wasn't sure that you'd agree to pose. I really do appreciate it."

Courtney smiled graciously. "You're welcome, KC."

Lauren didn't have much time. *Weekly Journal* editor Greg Sukamaki was breathing down her neck as she sat in the newspaper office that same afternoon, poring over her and Dash's hazing article.

"Is it ready?" Greg pushed.

"Just about. I just have to do a final proof."

"Well, do it," Greg barked. "We need a copy-ready paper early this week, because of vacation. If you want that article in the next issue, have it on my desk by four o'clock today."

"But, Greg—"

"Just have it there."

"All right. I will."

After Greg left, Lauren offered him a mock salute. Then she put her head back down and stared at the text while activity in the office bubbled around her. At the next desk two sportswriters were arguing over the merits of the basketball lineup, while a junior named Janet Benoit was yelling into a telephone.

"Look, I write an objective food column, not an advertisement for restaurants," Janet was hollering in a shrill soprano voice. "It's not my fault if your paella was too dry."

Lauren put her hands over her ears, but Janet's voice still intruded. So she scooped up the article and left the office to look for peace and quiet.

"Where am I supposed to go?" she asked herself.

Finally, she settled in the closest, quiet place—

the stairwell between the *Journal's* office and the building's first floor.

For at least twenty minutes not one person traveled up or down the stairs. Lauren congratulated herself as she got almost the entire article proofed. When she was down to the last paragraph, she heard the door open at the top of the stairs and the sound of light footsteps trotting down.

Lauren barely looked up, but when she heard the footsteps stall, she raised her eyes and her stomach clenched.

"Oh."

"Hi!" It was Christopher Hammond.

He was wearing a sport coat and loosened tie. His handsome face was ruddy, his auburn hair tousled, as if he'd jogged over. He sat down next to Lauren as if she were his oldest friend.

Lauren stared down at her paper. She was flooded with horrible memories of how she'd been set up with Christopher during orientation week, how she'd allowed herself to believe that he actually liked her. She also remembered the incredible humiliation when she'd realized that their date was all a hoax.

"You working on an article?" he asked in a warm, casual tone.

"Are you headed for the newspaper office?" Lauren tossed back. "It's right down there."

"No." Christopher smiled. "Actually, I came to see you."

Lauren suddenly wondered if he wanted information about Faith. She felt his shoulder touch hers. She fumbled. "Oh. Um, what about?"

He leaned across her lap and looked at her article. "Is that story ready to go to press?"

Lauren didn't have the presence of mind to hide her pages. "Yes."

Christopher didn't try to grab them away, or even read the print. "I've heard about it already."

"What?"

He smiled. "I know you got a scoop on a hazing incident that some guys in my house are responsible for. That's what I wanted to talk to you about."

Lauren wondered who had leaked news of her and Dash's story.

"You know, Lauren," he said, leaning forward and gesturing with his hands, "I've been trying to stop hazing for a long time. When I heard about what happened to Howard Benmann, I blew my stack. I can assure you that the guys who hazed Howard Benmann are on probation. They will each have to do twenty-five hours of community service."

"Really?"

Christopher nodded. "And after that, we still don't know if we'll let them back in the house. I just wanted to make sure you were writing about both sides of this issue. All I want is fairness. That's all."

Lauren wondered if Christopher was telling the truth. She also wondered if he knew that his name was in the article, as the interfraternity officer who had looked the other way.

He slid even closer.

Lauren blushed.

"Lauren, I understand why you wrote this article, and I agree that it's important to publish it. I just don't understand why you didn't interview us first to find out our side of things."

Lauren was beginning to think he had a point. She and Dash were so excited about getting a scoop that they hadn't bothered to find out the Greek's position. "You may be right. But I'm afraid it's too late now. If you want, you can always submit your own article later."

He nodded. "You're right. But I'd rather set the record straight now."

Lauren breathed in his after-shave and started to feel a little dizzy. It wasn't that she liked Christopher, or that she was interested in a relationship with any guy besides Dash. It was just that Christopher was the kind of guy every girl dreamed about from the time she realized that guys existed.

Lauren forced herself to inch away. "I don't think I can change anything in this article, Christopher. There isn't time. This is going in the next issue, so I guess you'll just have to submit a response to the editor if you have something you want to say."

Christopher put his face in his hands and was silent for a long time.

Lauren was just about to ask him if he was all right when he sat back up and grabbed her wrist.

"Do you think I'm really that worried about this article?" he said in a strange, intense voice.

"I . . . don't know," she stammered. "That's what it sounds like."

"Well, you're wrong. I'll tell you what really bothers me." He pulled her close to him, reached up, and took off her glasses. "What really bothers me is that you didn't come to me and tell me about this first. That hurts me, Lauren."

"It does?"

Lauren wasn't sure what was going on. She was scared and confused and completely off balance.

"You are so lovely," he whispered, leaning in to kiss her neck.

Lauren gasped.

"I know the Dream Date was a disaster," Christopher said, looking deep into Lauren's eyes. "I'm really sorry if you were hurt. But you've got to believe me when I say that I was very attracted to you. And I've been meaning to tell you just that ever since you helped me get the story for the TV station."

Lauren began to come back to earth. She sensed that Christopher was lying. He had to be lying! She was beginning to realize that almost every word that had come out of his mouth was an out-and-out lie. All he wanted was for her to stop her article.

But his kisses continued, and Lauren couldn't quite catch her breath. When he got to her mouth, she meant to turn away, she meant to push him away, but her lips parted and she leaned in. Her hand slipped onto his shoulder and she kissed him back.

In the middle of the kiss Lauren heard a blurry *tap, tap, tap* and was vaguely aware that someone else was traveling down the stairs. But it wasn't until she had pushed Christopher away and looked up that she recognized who it was.

"Dash!"

Dash was staring down at her, his dark eyes full of hurt and rage.

Lauren slammed Christopher with the flat of

her hand. She shot to her feet. "Dash . . . I . . ." She grabbed her glasses out of Christopher's hand and straightened her skirt.

"Save it," Dash spat out. "I know what's going on. Go back to your sorority and leave me alone."

Dash gave Lauren a searing, disgusted look, turned on his heels, and went back up the stairs.

Eleven

"ere's to midterms," toasted KC. "May they rest in peace."

"Here's to the White Rabbit and vacation and no dorm food for the next four days," Faith cheered.

"Here's to KC making a fortune with Matthew's calendar."

"I'll drink to that, Win," said KC.

Winnie laughed. "Here's to thanking Lauren for the use of her Beamer. And here's to getting away with meeting two fabulous, incredible guys on the same night, having another chance with both of them, and hoping it's not my last!"

Faith, Winnie, and KC turned their heads,

looking to the fourth and fifth members of their Wednesday night dining commons party. But neither Melissa nor Lauren was in a celebratory mood. Lauren stared down at her dinner as if it were poisoned, while Melissa gazed at the mountains out the big picture window.

"Melissa?" Winnie prompted, holding up her coffee cup. "What's your toast? This is our first college vacation. For the next four days you won't have to think about chemistry tables or track times or trying to live with all the pieces of stale cookie I leave around our room."

Melissa seemed preoccupied, but she finally offered a weak smile. She lifted her glass of milk and didn't look at anyone. "Here's to vacation," she said blandly.

Winnie, KC, and Faith exchanged confused glances.

Faith stared at Melissa for a moment longer, hesitated, then turned back to Lauren. "Lauren, what about you?"

Lauren seemed even more glum than Melissa. She pushed her wire-rimmed glasses against her face and didn't say a word.

"Come on, Lauren," prodded KC. "You have more to celebrate than any of us." She raised her glass again. "Here's to getting kicked out of the Tri Betas."

Winnie and Faith clinked.

"Here's to freedom from your mother!"

Winnie and Faith hooted.

KC cheered harder. "Here's to giving away all your stuff. Here's to getting your hazing article in the next issue of the newspaper and winning a Pulitzer prize!"

Lauren gave out a little groan, took off her glasses, and rested her head in her hands.

Faith patted Lauren, and for a while they all stared at her. When Lauren refused to lift her head, they all went back to their dinner.

"It's kind of empty in here," Winnie commented.

KC and Faith nodded.

Many students had already gone home, leaving only a third of the tables in the dorm dining commons filled. There were suitcases stacked in the foyer. It even seemed like the kitchen was eager to get cleaned out for the week. They'd served a variety of leftovers—meat loaf, macaroni and cheese, Swiss steak, and the taco casserole they'd served the night before.

"Lauren, what's the matter?" Winnie asked, unable to ignore Lauren's desperate mood. "You aren't sorry about getting kicked out of the Tri Betas, are you?"

Lauren shook her head as if Winnie's suggestion were the most absurd thing on earth. "It's not that."

"Well, what is it?"

Lauren sat up again and picked at her food. "I'm just a fool, that's all. I thought I'd changed so much since I'd written for the paper and even taken part in that demonstration with the Progressive Students Coalition. But I haven't changed. I'm still the same old stupid fool."

"Lauren, don't say that," Faith soothed.

"What happened?" Winnie asked.

Lauren took a long drink of water, as if to bolster her courage. She cleaned her glasses and put them back on. "Dash and I kind of had . . . well . . . it wasn't really a fight. I don't know what it was. I guess you could call it . . . a misunderstanding."

"Can you clear it up?" asked Faith.

"Clear it up right away," Winnie advised. "That's what my mother says. Never let things fester. Those are her words, needless to say."

"I don't know," Lauren mumbled. "I don't know if I can clear it up. It was my own dumb fault."

"Well," Winnie chattered when Lauren refused to elaborate, "for the next four days don't think about it and maybe by the time you get back from San Francisco on Monday, things will start to get worked out. That's my attitude, not my mother's. I've decided that if you're patient enough, anything can work out. Even me and Josh."

Lauren didn't look convinced.

"Win," KC said, "I thought you didn't know if Josh was the one or if Travis was?"

"Did I just say me and Josh and not mention Travis at all?" Winnie marveled. "Hmm. I wonder what my mother would say about that."

"Don't think about it," KC advised.

Winnie shrugged. "I think Lauren should do the same thing. Don't think about it. Think about your Thanksgiving turkey pig out instead."

"Think about stuffing," agreed KC.

Winnie licked her lips. "Think about those gross sweet potatoes with little marshmallows melted over the top. Think about how everyone gets together to eat early in the afternoon, and then by five o'clock you're all so stuffed that you never want to eat again!"

Lauren dropped her napkin over her tray. She looked even more defeated. "You know, I've never been to that kind of Thanksgiving," she admitted in a dull voice.

"What other kind of Thanksgiving is there?" asked Faith.

"Yeah," agreed Winnie. "I thought eating too much was an American tradition."

KC laughed. "That and seeing all the relatives you barely see the rest of the year."

Melissa looked up, flinched, and then pushed her tray away, too.

"I've usually had Thanksgivings in embassies or restaurants or hotels, or at one of my boarding schools," Lauren said.

"Really?" Faith asked, surprised. "You mean you've never eaten turkey leftovers in sandwiches? Or turkey soup and cold stuffing for breakfast?"

"No."

"You always went out to restaurants on Thanksgiving?" KC pressed.

"KC, it's not that weird," Winnie interrupted. "We're all going out to a restaurant this Thanksgiving. Your parents' restaurant."

"That's different. My parents' restaurant will be closed, except for us and our families. It'll be just like having it at home, only with more room and even better food."

Faith smiled. "I can't wait. KC, your mother makes the best pumpkin pie in the entire West."

"Pecan pie, too," KC said, drooling. "With fresh whipped cream."

KC and Faith moaned.

Winnie leaned in toward her two best friends. "So okay you two, what else are we going to do while we're home?"

"Check out the new movies at the fourplex theater," Faith decided, getting carried away with anticipation.

"Do a supermarket-sweep shopping spree on Friday at the mall," said KC.

"Go by the high school and relive old times." Winnie giggled.

"I can't believe how much I'm actually looking forward to seeing my folks." KC grinned. "I think holidays like Thanksgiving bring out the best in them."

"Your folks are always at their best, KC," said Winnie. "Like offering to make dinner for all of us. That is so cool. My mom always says how generous and well balanced your parents are. I can't wait to be home!"

Faith nodded. "I'm even looking forward to seeing Marlee and my folks, even after how weird they were when they came here on parents' weekend. I want to talk to them some more and see how Marlee's getting along. I'm actually kind of homesick."

"I guess being away from home makes you appreciate your family a lot more," KC said.

All three of them nodded, then fell quiet as they noticed that Lauren had grown gloomy again and Melissa had begun tearing her napkin into little shreds.

"Of course, there are all kinds of Thanksgivings," Winnie said, backtracking. "I'm sure a Thanksgiving dinner in a great hotel in London or Tokyo beats turkey in Jacksonville any day."

Lauren tried to smile, although she was no longer the gloomiest girl at the table. Melissa wasn't just shredding her napkin, she looked like she was holding back tears. Her face had turned white under her freckles. Her mouth was a tight line, and her eyes were hidden behind her hand. Suddenly she shoved back her chair and grabbed her workout bag.

"Excuse me," Melissa mumbled.

Winnie looked up. "Melissa, are you okay?"

"I have to go."

"Are you going back to the room?" Winnie blurted. "Will I see you before I leave to meet Travis tonight?"

Melissa didn't answer. She ran out at top speed.

Even Lauren looked up to watch Melissa sprint through the dining commons and out the door. Once Melissa was gone, the four girls looked at one another.

"What did I say?" Winnie asked.

KC and Lauren shrugged.

"I don't think it had anything to do with you," Faith decided.

"What did it have to do with?" Winnie asked.

"I don't know," Faith said, suddenly acting as gloomy as Lauren. "Melissa McDormand is a mystery to me."

Melissa ducked into the pantry that was right next to the kitchen. Surrounded by institution-sized containers of mustard and pickles and huge packages of paper napkins, she turned her face to the wall. The place was cold. It smelled of dried onion and salt, but Melissa couldn't have made it much farther. Besides, the pantry served her purpose. She wanted to weep in peace.

"Shut up, all of you! I don't want to hear any more," Melissa sobbed.

Melissa couldn't bear any more stories of lovely Thanksgivings. She didn't want to think about homemade cranberry sauce and sweet potatoes, extended families and great trips home. She didn't even want to know about Lauren's miserable Thanksgivings at fancy hotels. And most of all, she didn't want anyone to see her cry.

Melissa huddled into a little nook and let the tears flow. She wasn't a crybaby, but this time the tears were unstoppable. The sobs came out in a horrendous, embarrassing rush.

Melissa didn't try to stop the tears until she heard footsteps and a voice outside the pantry door.

"Melissa?"

She froze.

"Melissa, what's wrong?"

Melissa looked over through blurry eyes and then groaned. The last person she'd wanted to see her in this state had just entered the pantry doorway.

"Not you," she moaned.

Brooks Baldwin stared.

"Go away."

"I'm not going anywhere," he said right back.

Melissa wouldn't look at him, but she sensed that he was moving even closer. "Where did you come from, anyway!" she asked, going on the attack. "What do you do, hide in corners so you can jump out and surprise me when I least expect it?"

He shook his head. "I was sitting in the dining commons with Barney, my roommate. You didn't see me, but I saw you run out. I followed you to make sure you were okay."

"I'm okay!"

"You don't look okay."

Melissa's head hurt and she was tired. In spite of herself she lifted her head and looked into Brooks's caring face.

He reached out to dab her tears, but she

flinched so he put his hand down. "I've been wanting to talk to you anyway."

"We talked at the gym."

"That wasn't exactly what I would call a satisfying conversation."

Melissa took a deep breath. Part of her was grateful that Brooks had found her—incredibly grateful—just like part of her had been overjoyed when he'd come to talk to her in the gym. But another part of her wanted to run, to hide, to never see Brooks again.

"Listen," she said, trying to squeeze past him, "I have to go. I have a lot of homework to do."

"Melissa!" Brooks stopped her. "Look, if I'm bugging you, just tell me. Tell me to leave you alone, tell me you think I'm a creep, tell me you don't ever want to go out with me or talk to me again and I promise, I'll leave you alone."

Melissa didn't say anything.

"But don't give me this craziness about having to study," Brooks went on. "Nobody has to study the night before Thanksgiving vacation. Nobody has to work so hard every single second that they never have time to go out or do anything else."

Melissa wanted to go on the attack again, but something about Brooks made her want to open up. She sank down and sat on a huge cardboard box.

"Anyway," Brooks said in a softer voice, "I wanted to give this one more chance. I wanted to ask you what you were doing over Thanksgiving. I know you live in town here, and you probably have plans. But I thought you might like to spend Thanksgiving with me and my parents. We could come back on Friday. I actually plan on coming back that early to coach some local kids in soccer."

When Melissa didn't respond, he said. "What did I do wrong now? Is it an insult to ask you to my Thanksgiving?"

"Why is everybody so obsessed with Thanksgiving?" Melissa ranted. "It's just a stupid four-day holiday where nothing happens except that school stops so we have to go home. But we don't do anything once we get there. It's just a waste of time."

"So maybe people need to waste time after working hard," Brooks reasoned, even though he looked confused. "They need to see all their aunts and uncles and all those second and third cousins whose names they can't remember."

"Well, some of us don't have second cousins or aunts or uncles who come over and visit. Some of us don't have Thanksgiving at all!"

Brooks stepped in and grabbed Melissa's arms, and she knew she had said too much. She wasn't sure how or why it had slipped out, except that it had been in her mind so much over the last week. She felt herself lean toward Brooks, while at the same time she wanted to push him away.

"What are you saying? Don't you have a family?" he asked.

Melissa felt the pull of tears again. "Sure, I have a family. Everyone has a family."

He kept hold of her and waited.

"Do you want to know what a wonderful Thanksgiving I'm going to have?" she finally said. "My mother won't be there because she'll have to work as a housekeeper, cleaning up and serving someone else's Thanksgiving, which means that either I make the dinner, which is a total joke because I can't fry a hamburger, or we just forget the whole thing, like we've done every year. My dad will be drunk the whole time anyway, and my brother will probably forget to show up."

Brooks slipped his arms all the way around her. He sighed. "I'm sorry," he said.

"Don't feel sorry for me," she argued, half-heartedly pushing him away. "I hate it when people feel sorry for me, and there's nothing to feel sorry for. It's just the way it is."

"So why do you go home at all?"

For one moment, Melissa allowed herself to let Brooks comfort her. "What else am I supposed to do? Stay alone in the dorms? Take a trip to London or Rome on my American Express card?"

"You could come to Jacksonville with me."

She pulled back and looked into his face as tears rolled down her cheeks again. "What?"

"You could come to Thanksgiving with my family. We could go there together. It's nothing special, just the normal turkey and trimmings with my dad and my stepmother, my grandparents, and some other family and friends."

"I don't think so."

Brooks gently put a finger to her lips. "Look, you don't have to answer right now or decide this second. I'll leave you a note in your room with all the info about how to get there and where to meet me. The important thing is that you know I want you to come. Will you remember that? I'd like you to join us."

Melissa nodded. She stood close to him a little longer, then pushed him back to arm's length and ran back to her dorm.

Twelve

....

Winnie turned into The Beanery's parking lot and found an empty spot for Lauren's BMW. She shut the engine off but held on to the steering wheel.

"Love," Winnie said with a sigh as she leaned over the wheel and pulled up the emergency brake. She was trying to fight those old impulsive, I'll-do-anything Winnie feelings again, but it seemed to be a losing battle. She knew she was getting crazy again, because now that she was on her way to her big, make-it-or-break-it date with Travis, she couldn't stop thinking about Josh. Whenever Winnie thought about one of them, she always got swept up in the moment and put the other out of her mind.

At first Winnie had been overjoyed by the idea of Travis showing up again. She'd been excited by the notion of two fabulous guys being interested in her. But now things seemed to be getting complicated.

"What am I going to do?" she whispered, realizing just what an insane dilemma she was in.

She was remembering when she'd gone too fast and thrown herself at Josh her first week at U of S. Josh had played it cool, though, and he hadn't taken advantage of her, even when Winnie had gotten drunk and passed out in his room. Instead, he'd covered her with a blanket and looked after her. He'd been a little cautious. He'd held back.

Travis, on the other hand, liked living in a speeded-up world. There was no such thing as going too fast for him, or taking too big a risk. But now that Winnie was feeling speeded up again, it scared her. She liked the little caution she had introduced into her life. She liked college and the dorms and living down the hall from Josh.

She realized she would have to be cautious and careful that night. She couldn't overstay her time with Travis. Especially not if she wanted to meet Josh at ten-thirty to clear things up and slowly start over again. By eleven-thirty she would have to be on her way to the bus station, in time to meet Faith and KC and catch the midnight bus home.

Winnie slammed the door of the BMW and patted the glossy, white paint, assuring herself that she wouldn't have to worry about getting back across town this time. She wasn't going to mess up. She wasn't going to be late. The new Beamer was reliable. Winnie had even mapped out the entire route home ahead of time so that nothing could mess up and get in her way.

Trying to steady herself with a deep breath, Winnie walked across the gravel parking lot and into the coffeehouse to meet the other guy in her life. The thick wooden door was heavy, but once open, the smell of rich coffee, perfume, chocolate, and cinnamon wafted into the night air. The lights inside were low and the conversations were at a pleasant murmur. As Winnie waited for a table, she heard the strum of a twangy acoustic guitar.

She walked farther into the main room of the coffeehouse and saw Travis up on the small stage. His long hair was pulled back in a ponytail. He was wearing a vest he'd bought in Belgium and a pair of soft, baggy pants. When he spotted her, he did a little bow, sending her a smile that was meant only for her.

Then he sat on the tall wooden stool and leaned over to adjust the microphone. "I'm Travis Bennett," he said. "And I'm glad to be here. This first song is for a special friend. She knows who she is."

Winnie sank into a chair.

Travis began to sing in his husky, mellow voice. Listening to him was like swinging in a musical hammock on a hot, summer's day. The song was sad, about a girl he'd met in a faraway place, a girl who'd given so much, then taken herself away just as completely.

People sat forward as Travis's song went on. Chatter stopped. Coffee cups were lowered more carefully and waitresses bent low to hear orders that were whispered in their ears.

Winnie began to weep. She'd forgotten the magical quality of Travis's singing voice, the way he made her feel that every word he sang was absolutely true.

"Would you like to order?" whispered a waitress who barely looked at Winnie. Even she was too busy watching Travis.

Winnie pressed a napkin to her eyes. "Espresso," she said, remembering the long night she had ahead of her. She began to realize that she was ready to say good-bye to Travis, and that was why she was crying. She couldn't throw herself back into the middle of July as if no time had passed. And she couldn't block out thoughts of Josh anymore.

Travis sang four more songs. One was about traveling on trains, another about lost love. Then he sang an oldie and a funny tune written by a friend of his. At the end of Travis's set there was a swell of applause.

"Thank you one and all," Travis said, taking off his guitar and smiling at the crowd. He stayed up on the stage while the man who owned The Beanery trotted up and whispered something in his ear. Travis nodded and then leaned into the microphone again. "Folks, I've just been asked to sing another set later tonight, so I hope you'll all stick around to listen. Thanks again. You were a great audience."

There was more applause and a few whistles as Travis climbed off the stage. On his way through the coffeehouse three or four people stopped him to tell him how much they'd liked his songs.

Finally he sat down at Winnie's small, round table. He ordered soda, then leaned over the table and took Winnie's hand.

"Hi," Travis whispered.

"Hi."

"You look beautiful."

Winnie suddenly felt like she was back in Paris

again, going on one of Travis's whirlwind tours, falling into his arms as they climbed the spiral staircase that led back to his hotel room.

"I'm not beautiful," she said, self-consciously patting her spiky hair.

"Of course you are." His eyes took in every inch of her face. "I'm glad you made it."

"Did you think I wouldn't come?"

Travis cocked his head and sipped his soda. "I had some doubts. Just an instinct, but my instincts are usually right."

Winnie wondered if Travis sensed, just as she did, that their romance was not going to be revived. "Travis, I've had to study over the last few days. That's the only reason why I haven't seen you."

"I know. But I'm an all or nothing person, Win. In Paris I thought you were the same way."

"I was."

"But you're not anymore."

Winnie didn't respond. The next musical act had taken the stage, a duet that sang folk songs in sweet harmony.

"Are you, Win?"

Winnie thought about even-tempered, charming Josh again. She thought about her classes, her friends, her new life. In Paris she'd wanted Travis to change her life, but now she was beginning to be happy with life just the way it was. If there were changes to be made, she wanted to make them herself.

"Win, you haven't answered me," Travis prodded.

Winnie took a deep breath. "I don't know. Sometimes I want to still be like the girl you knew in Paris, but being like that got me into so much trouble, Travis. As much as it made me feel wonderful sometimes, and as much as I had great adventures, it also made me feel terrible and I made awful messes of things."

"That's what life is about, Win," Travis said.

Winnie shook her head and her long earrings swung. "Is it? When we were together in Paris I felt so happy, as happy as I think I've ever been."

Travis smiled.

"But when you left, I was so lonely I didn't know what to do. And then I didn't hear from you and I was so depressed that I thought I would never make it back to the States alive."

Travis nodded.

"After that I went from being happy, to lonely, to depressed. Even my first few weeks here I was bouncing off the walls from one emotion to another. I don't want to be that way again. If I go to extremes all the time I'll never find out who I am and what I'm good at."

Travis reached over and clutched her hands. "I think I understand what you're saying. I get the message." He sat back and sipped his soda for a while, watching the duet and tapping his foot. "Will you stay for my late set?" he finally asked.

Winnie was tempted. She thought it might be the last time she'd ever see Travis. Still, she made herself think about Josh. She thought about KC and Faith waiting for her at the bus stop, and about Thanksgiving dinner. She thought about college and her future. Travis might think of all that as a compromise, but to her, classes and friends, family and hopefully Josh were what it was all about. "I can't. I'm sorry. I have to go by ten . . . to get to the bus station to meet Faith and KC."

Travis stared at her for a long time before leaning back over the table and grabbing her hand again. "Win, you know me. I don't stand still for long. If this isn't going to be the real thing, then I'll move on soon. I have to go to LA anyway if I'm going to try and make it in the music business. And I do want to make it. I feel like all or nothing is the way to go with my music, too."

Winnie nodded. "Your music is incredible. You should go to LA. I know you'll get a record contract."

"Thanks." Travis looked down. "I was going to ask you to come with me, Win."

"To LA?"

He nodded.

"What would I do in LA?"

Travis shrugged. "You'd figure that out when you got there."

Winnie had to smile. It was so like Travis to pop into her life, disappear, reappear again, then expect her to pack up and disappear with him. The extreme part of her was tempted—but that part didn't tip the scales anymore. "Travis, now that I hear you sing again, I know that your life is your music."

Travis grinned. He took Winnie's hand and kissed it. "I knew you believed in me. And I know I'll make it if you come with me. I can feel it. My instinct tells me that this is the right thing to do. We'll leave this weekend."

"Travis!" Winnie leaned over the table and touched his face. "Travis, I can't leave this weekend. I can't leave at all."

"But Win—"

"My life is here."

Travis collapsed a little and got a faraway look. "Are you sure? Win, I'll leave this weekend no matter what. If you don't come with me, then this is it. I need you, Win."

Winnie took in every inch of his face. She memorized the sound of his voice and the way he leaned in his chair for old times' sake. "You won't need me in LA," she said. "You'll make it, no matter what."

When Winnie walked out of The Beanery a short while later, she knew that she had made it, too. She had plenty of time to get back to the dorms by ten-thirty. She felt calm. She was sure that Travis was choosing the right path for his life by heading to LA, and that she was doing the same by staying exactly where she was.

"Congratulations, Ms. Gottlieb," she told herself as she climbed back in Lauren's car and started the engine. The BMW roared. Winnie eased off the gas, opened her window, and put the car in gear.

It was a clear night. Cold, still, and dry. Even in the dark, Winnie felt confident and secure as she pulled out of The Beanery parking lot and carefully followed her route back to the dorms. She stuck a tape in Lauren's tape player, and after she passed the center of downtown Springfield, she turned the volume up high.

Winnie tapped the steering wheel. She bobbed in her seat. She felt so good about her newfound maturity that she wanted to fly the Beamer into orbit and take a cruise around the universe. The tune over the tape player was peppy and hot. She felt the same way inside—strong, spirited, sexy, and in tune.

She began to sing along in an off-key voice.

Out of the blue.
Out of the wilderness.
I came to the other side, to find you oo ooo.

Winnie threw back her head as she approached the last light before campus, a light that was notorious for taking an eternity to change. As she reached it, the green turned to yellow.

"Okay," Winnie sang, stepping on the brakes. She stopped and waited, and waited, as the light took its leisurely time. Then she stepped on the gas the split second the light turned green, and lurched forward.

That was when Winnie saw a flash of light, a panel of red. Her heart leapt into her mouth and her pulse went wild.

"AHHHH!!!" Winnie gasped.

For a moment she didn't know what was going on. Then she saw it more clearly, as if in slow motion. A red pickup was racing from the other direction, trying to make it through even though the last second of yellow light was long gone. Winnie caught a glimpse of the young man driving. He had twisted up his face and hunched his shoulders, and he looked as terrified and out of control as she felt.

"STOP!" she screamed.

And that's when she felt a thrust from the side. There was the horrible screech of smashed metal and the endless crash of broken glass. Winnie was shoved sideways in her shoulder harness, and her head smacked against the steering wheel. She felt a searing line of pain from her forehead to her ear.

"OH, GOD," Winnie heard someone wail.

And just as she realized that the cry had come from herself, she felt something wet and warm streaming down the side of her face. She lifted her hand, held it in front of her, and saw blood in the moonlight. Her head began to throb and her stomach turned over. Winnie's whole body broke into a sweat, and then everything went black.

Thirteen

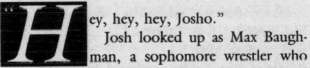

"**H**ey, hey, hey, Josho."

Josh looked up as Max Baugh-man, a sophomore wrestler who also lived in Forest Hall, clapped his hands and did a little dance.

"Hey, Max," Josh responded flatly.

Max took a beer can from behind his back, swigged it, and hid it behind his back again.

"What's up, Max?"

"Good question, Josho. Many things are up. So what are you doing sitting in the lobby all by yourself? It's party time. It's the boogie-woogie hour."

"Yeah?"

"Josho, why don't you come upstairs? There's hardly anybody left in this lousy dorm, but everybody that's anybody is joining the blowout in my room."

Josh had figured there was a party going on upstairs. He'd heard the foot stomping and the laughter through the lobby ceiling. The sound of it had been like someone whapping a piece of wood against his head. "Sorry, Max," Josh said. "I've got other plans."

"Yeah. I see," Max goaded.

Josh stared straight ahead.

Max guffawed. "Like sitting alone down here and twiddling your thumbs."

"I'm okay, Max."

"Yeah, sure." Max tinkered with the light switch. "Why don't you take a nap. You'll probably still be sitting on that same sofa when we all get back on Monday."

"Very funny," Josh muttered.

Max took another swig and wiped his mouth with the back of his hand. "So, Josho, what are you doing for vacation?"

"Visiting friends."

"You're not going home?"

Josh shook his head. "My dad's in the military. He and my mom are stationed in Germany. I'll see them over Christmas."

"I wish my parents were in Germany," Max cracked. "But no such luck. I'm leaving tomorrow morning." He offered a sip of his beer to Josh. When Josh refused, Max shook his head and lumbered back over to the stairs. "I'll only say it one more time, Josho boy. Come on up."

"Maybe later."

Max bent down for one last barb. "What are you doing down here, anyway?"

Josh sat motionless until Max was gone. Then he sighed. "Good question. What am I doing down here?"

Josh had been waiting for almost half an hour. He didn't know why he had waited so long. And all he knew was that he wouldn't be there much longer.

"I can't believe you did this to me again, Winnie," Josh groaned. "You must think I'm the biggest sucker in the world. And you may be right."

Josh slugged the seat of the sofa. Actually, he didn't think of himself as a sucker. He thought of himself as an independent kind of person, someone who was open to life as it happened, someone who could go with the flow. When he'd first arrived at the U of S, Winnie had come on so strong that he'd been hesitant. He'd liked her immediately, but he'd gotten the feeling that Winnie had tons of boyfriends. She'd given him the impression that she flirted with guys just for the kick of it, then went on her merry way. And so Josh had kept his distance.

But in recent weeks, Josh had run into Winnie every once in a while. Every time he saw her, he realized that he liked her more and more. She had a goofy smile and a smart gleam in her eyes, as if she wanted to attack freshman year and relish every moment.

Josh had fallen for her.

Winnie, however, didn't seem to care. She'd stood him up for their date. And now that he'd given her a second chance, she was throwing it in his face.

Being easygoing was one thing, Josh decided.

Being a royal chump was another.

An hour later, the bus station in downtown Springfield was anything but easygoing. Announcements blared. Video games pinged. Lights flickered. Students lugged duffel bags and exchanged horror stories about midterms. Buses honked and chugged off for points north and south, leaving big clouds of exhaust behind.

Faith and KC clutched their vacation gear and hurried into line for the midnight Jacksonville bus.

"Where is Winnie!" Faith said worriedly.

"That's the million-dollar question," said KC.

Faith checked her watch. "Do you think she'll make it?"

"Of course she'll make it," KC assured her as they found their way outside the terminal and onto the platform. They located the bus bound for Jacksonville and let the bus driver take their luggage to stow it away. "At least I hope Winnie makes it."

"Me, too."

KC held their tickets out and they both climbed on.

"Why do these buses always smell so gross?" Faith asked as she sidled down the narrow aisle. The bus was already crowded. Faith hoisted her book bag over her head and made her way farther back.

KC was following right behind. "I don't know. But when I get rich, I think I'll only travel by private plane."

"Will you take me along?"

"Absolutely."

Students were sprawled across the first seven or eight rows. Using sweaters as blankets, many read or pretended to be asleep so that no one would occupy the seat next to them.

"Let's grab these," Faith said, when she reached the first empty row near the back. She sat next to the window and put her fringed suede jacket on the seat next to her. Meanwhile, KC stretched out on the double seat across the aisle.

"We'll save a seat for Winnie."

"Two seats. One for Winnie, and one for her junk." Faith turned and pressed her face to the glass. "I still don't see her! What could be keeping her? The bus leaves in a few minutes."

KC got up on her knees to look out, too. "Knowing Winnie she'll probably get here just as the bus is pulling out."

"Really." Faith tried to smile. "And the driver will slam on his brakes to pick her up."

KC nodded. "I just hope she makes it."

"I just hope she's okay."

"She's okay," KC declared after giving it a moment's thought. "In spite of the way she acted last week when you drove her down here to meet Travis, I think she's getting it together. Well, at least she seemed like she was getting it together, until Travis arrived."

"I know." Faith thought for a moment, too. Then she threw up her hands. "What are we going to do if she doesn't show up?"

KC frowned. "What can we do? Maybe she found a ride. Maybe things with Josh worked out so well that she couldn't tear herself away. I'm worried, too, but all we can do is assume that Winnie will show up before this bus leaves."

Faith finally sighed and pulled out her *Alice in Wonderland* script, looking up frequently as students continued to make their way onto the bus carrying backpacks and sleeping bags and books. One by one they filled the remaining seats, while Faith and KC used all the power of their body language to try to save both of their extra seats for Winnie.

Faith tensed up when someone tapped her shoulder. She considered ignoring him, until she heard his voice.

"Is someone sitting here?"

Faith looked up and saw blond curls and an easy smile. She even recognized the red cable-knit sweater, since her mother had given it to him for his sixteenth birthday.

"Brooks."

"Faith. Hey."

"Hi." Faith didn't know why she was so surprised to see him. Everything inside her body suddenly felt alive. Of course Brooks would also be heading back to Jacksonville for a family Thanksgiving, she told herself. Then she remembered Thanksgivings they had shared in the past and smiled. "Do you want to sit here?"

He checked out the seats behind them. They were almost all full. "Can I?"

Faith moved her jacket. "Sure."

"Hi, Brooks," said KC from the other side of the aisle. "We're waiting for Winnie. We saved her two seats because she always has so much stuff. But it looks like it's going to be too crowded to save extra seats."

Brooks laughed. He took a sports magazine out of his athletic bag, then tossed the bag up onto the overhead rack.

"If Winnie makes it, that is," Faith added. "She's late."

Brooks sat down next to Faith. "Sounds like Winnie." He smiled.

Faith realized that she was glad for this accidental meeting. She liked the idea of Brooks's company on the long, late-night ride home. There was still a lot of misunderstanding to clear up between them, and maybe this would be the time to set every last thing right.

"Brooks, you just made it yourself," Faith said, pleased to feel so comfortable making small talk. For such a long time after the breakup, they'd been unable to even exchange pleasantries. And after her intense, secretive romance with Christopher Hammond, it felt good to be around a guy who was a straightforward friend. "And being late isn't like you. From what I remember, you used to always get places at least fifteen minutes ahead of time."

"Still do." Brooks tapped his magazine against his thigh. "I even got here early tonight. I was inside the station, waiting for somebody I thought might meet me. But they didn't show up." He stared down at his hands, then shrugged. "So I decided I'd better get a seat before the bus left without me."

Faith wondered if Brooks had been waiting for his roommate, Barney Sharfenburger, or for someone else from his dorm. "You didn't see Winnie by any chance, did you?"

"Sorry. I didn't." Brooks craned his neck to catch a glimpse of the window.

The bus driver climbed back onto the bus. He started the engine, then got up to count heads while the bus warmed up.

"Are you looking forward to being home?" Faith asked Brooks.

He didn't seem to hear her. He was watching the bus driver finish his paperwork and sit down behind the wheel. The door to the bus closed with an airy whoosh. "Hmm?"

"I bet you're looking forward to that great stuffing your mom makes, with the chestnuts."

He nodded, but Faith knew he still hadn't really heard her.

She thought about Winnie again. "I guess we're leaving. I guess Winnie didn't make it. I hate it when she does this! I hope she's okay. I hope she got some great ride and will be waiting at the station when we get to Jacksonville."

Brooks nodded blankly.

The driver adjusted his mirrors. He put the bus in gear and was just about to pull out when there was a frantic knock on the door.

"It's Winnie," cried KC.

Faith lunged forward, but could only see the bus driver leaning over to reopen the door.

"It has to be," Faith agreed with relief. "She's going to make one of her last-minute entrances."

Brooks sat forward, too, then he jumped to his feet.

Faith watched, openmouthed, as the late passenger handed her ticket to the bus driver.

It wasn't Winnie.

It was Melissa McDormand, and she slowly made her way down the aisle as if she wasn't sure she wanted to be there.

The bus began to move. Melissa steadied herself as she made her way back. Once she spotted Brooks she stood taller, and no matter how she lurched and lost her footing, her eyes didn't waver. Her gaze was stuck on Brooks.

Brooks took a few steps forward to help Melissa with her luggage since she had arrived too late to stow things under the bus. Melissa carried a cheap, heavy suitcase and a U of S gym bag. Brooks took the suitcase and lifted it, almost knocking into Faith.

Faith sank into her seat, feeling as if she'd just become invisible.

"Melissa, I'm so glad you decided to come," Brooks said. He grabbed Melissa's arms and helped her into the seat that KC had been saving for Winnie.

Melissa sat down. "I was afraid you wouldn't be here," she said, leaning across the aisle.

"Why?" said Brooks. "I left you a note telling you where to meet me. I thought you'd decided not to come."

"I almost didn't come. I couldn't believe you'd really want me to join your family. You barely know me."

"After this, I'll know you better."

Melissa smiled.

"You won't be sorry," Brooks promised Melissa. "You'll have a great time with us. My family will be really glad to have you join us." He took her hand and squeezed it.

Faith tried not to stare as Brooks then put his hand on the side of Melissa's face and gazed into her eyes. He leaned across the aisle and kissed Melissa, slowly, gently, the exact same way he'd kissed Faith a thousand times in the years they'd been together.

Faith knew that KC was trying to give her a sympathetic look, but she didn't even want her friend to see how uncomfortable she was. She turned toward the window. There was a knot in her stomach the size of a softball. She thought about Christopher and how Brooks had been forced to see her with another guy. She thought about how he must have felt and how sick she felt right then.

It wasn't that she wanted to be together with Brooks again. At least she didn't think she did. But she also didn't want to sit there for two hours while his new romance was thrown in her face. She wished that she could beam herself off the bus, or at least crawl under the seat.

Fourteen

t one-thirty A.M. Winnie was dropped
back at the U of S dorms.

"Are you sure you're okay? You're
not dizzy or seeing double?" asked Marjorie
Meyer, the policewoman who'd been with Winnie
off and on since the accident.

"They checked all that at the hospital," Winnie
said. "I kind of have a headache still, where I got
the bad cut. But I'm okay."

Officer Meyer parked her squad car in the emergency parking space right behind Forest Hall.

Winnie touched the bandage taped to her forehead. A little chunk of spiked hair had been

shaved away. She tried to pull her bangs over the wound. "Thank you. You've been really helpful."

"Hold on," said Officer Meyer, getting out of the car. "I'll walk you in."

Winnie slowly got out and waited for Marjorie to lock up the squad car. The doctors had made sure that Winnie didn't have a concussion. She did have a gash on her forehead, a scraped hand, sore neck, and various scrapes and bruises from her forearms to her knees. "Thanks. Gee, maybe I'll get famous," Winnie managed to joke as they went in the back door. "A freshman who deserves a police escort."

"You deserve something," Officer Meyer agreed. "You've had quite a night."

And you don't know the half of it, Winnie wanted to add. But she had no more energy for silly banter. She stayed by Marjorie's side until they were down the hall and in the Forest lobby.

The dorm lobby was empty, and there wasn't a sound to be heard. Winnie sat down on a sofa.

"You'll call your mother first thing?" Officer Meyer reminded.

Winnie nodded. "My bus wasn't supposed to get in until two, so my mom won't be worried. Actually, she's probably asleep. But I'll call her right away. Don't worry."

"Good girl."

Winnie looked around while Officer Meyer answered a call on her walkie-talkie. Suddenly the Forest Hall lobby looked like a foreign place to Winnie. She felt as out of place as she had the first day she'd arrived. Since the accident she'd been feeling dislocated and terribly homesick. She kept telling herself that she was in college now, that she shouldn't want her mother and her old bedroom back in Jacksonville. But those were exactly the two things she longed for.

After answering her call about a suspected burglary downtown, Officer Meyer put her walkie-talkie away and looked down at Winnie. "Now do you remember what to tell your friend, the one who owns the car?"

"I think so," Winnie said, feeling a little sick. "I don't think I'll call her tonight, though. It's so late and I think she just flew into San Francisco a few hours ago. I don't want to wake her and her uncle up with this kind of news."

Officer Meyer smiled. "You may have a point there."

Winnie touched her bandage again. She could just imagine calling some San Francisco mansion and waking everyone up to say, "Hi, Lauren. Remember your new BMW? Well, I trashed it. No joke. I really did. The tow truck driver said he thinks it's totaled. He took it down to some place called Mac's Foreign Auto, which wasn't open since the accident happened in the middle of the night. So, we left your Beamer in Mac's driveway and boy does that car look like a heap of junk. Sorry!" Winnie wanted to wipe the whole thing out of her memory.

"Are you sure you're okay?" Officer Meyer checked.

Winnie looked up. "Yeah. I was just thinking about breaking the crash news. Not a pretty thought."

Officer Meyer nodded.

"The accident wasn't my fault. Was it?"

"I'm not the one who decides that," said the officer, "but I will say that the other driver was speeding, and he ran a red light to boot. Don't worry." She patted Winnie's arm.

"Thanks."

"Well Winnie, unless you need something, I've got to be on my way." Officer Meyer looked around. "Is this place always this quiet?"

"I guess everybody's already gone for Thanksgiving vacation," Winnie explained.

Officer Meyer nodded. She waved and headed out the door.

"Thanks again," Winnie called after her. "Happy Thanksgiving."

After the back door closed, Winnie mumbled,

"Happy Thanksgiving. What a joke. How about horrible Thanksgiving. Horrendous Thanksgiving. Worst Thanksgiving of my life."

Winnie tried to laugh, but as soon as she let the emotion bubble out of her, she began to weep instead. For the first time since the crash, she cried without inhibition.

When she was all cried out, she sat up again. She calmed herself. She wiped away the little bit of makeup that was left to wipe away and took trembly breaths. Finally she stood up, searched her pockets and purse for change, and trudged up the stairs to her floor. She wandered down the hall to find the phone.

For a moment Winnie couldn't remember where her room was, let alone where the phone was, but she kept walking down the beige, overlit hall and soon she was there. She stacked her change on the shelf by the phone and punched in the number. When the operator told her how many coins to deposit, Winnie obeyed as if she were a robot. She waited through four rings.

Her mother's machine picked up.

"Hello," said the recording. *"You have reached the residence and office of Francine Gottlieb, specialist in family therapy. I can't take your call at the moment, but if you leave a message after the beep, I will be sure to call you back. If this is a crisis situation,*

please phone Dr. Ruth Garfield, who is on call at the Jacksonville Clinic, at 555-1254. Thank you. Good-bye."

Even though it was a recording, Winnie was comforted by the soothing sound of her mother's voice. And yet, hearing it made Winnie feel even more homesick and miserable about missing the bus and not being on her way home.

Beep.

"Um, hi, Mom," Winnie said. "I miss you. Listen, I'm not on the bus tonight with Faith and KC. Don't worry, but I got into a car accident in Faith's roommate's car. I'm okay. Honest. I'm not really hurt. I was driving, but it wasn't my fault. That's true, too. Anyway, I guess I'll get the first bus home tomorrow, but I don't think it leaves until two and it's that Podunk run, the one that stops about every five seconds, so I probably won't get home until after the dinner at KC's parents' restaurant is over. Go ahead without me. Tell everybody I'm okay and I miss them. Happy Thanksgiving. I love you. See you soon. Bye."

Winnie hung up and heard the coins clang and drop. She expected to start to cry again, but this time the tears didn't come. She just had a dark, empty feeling. Travis was gone. Things with Josh were ruined. And she wouldn't even see her mother until late the next night. Feeling defeated and weary, she padded back down the hall.

The dorm was eerily empty. Winnie usually had to hide from water ballooners or jocks who tried to tickle and harass her, but tonight the place reminded her of a haunted house. The silence echoed. The overhead fluorescent lights seemed to be alive, and the floor squeaked.

Winnie stopped at Josh's door. He was probably gone, but she was hoping that Mikoto might be there. She wanted to know that she wasn't going to be the only human in that big dorm that night.

Then she stared at the room number and thought about Josh again and went numb. How many times could someone mess up something so wonderful? she wondered. She was an all-time jerk, a hopeless, pathetic bumbler, an irresponsible airhead and a fool.

She knocked anyway, figuring that she had nothing left to lose. Once. Twice. She pounded hard, then didn't bother with a fourth knock. Even if Josh was there, what was she supposed to say to him? *Oh hi. I thought I'd wake you up in the middle of the night again. Sorry about our date— again. You see, I had a date with this other guy tonight, too, but I said good-bye to him. And actually, that had nothing to do with my being late. Not this time, anyway. This time it wasn't my fault, and you're really the one I care for anyway.*

"Pathetic," Winnie told herself. "You are truly pathetic."

She made her way farther down the hall and slowly unlocked the door to her own room.

The sight of her empty room just made her feel worse. Her carpetbags were ready and packed, waiting expectantly on the floor. Melissa's bed had been stripped and her anatomy models stared at Winnie like plastic demons.

"Don't stare, it's not polite," Winnie told the plastic woman whose organs were all labeled with bright red tags. Winnie turned the model around so it faced Melissa's typewriter. Then she grabbed her pillow and bedspread and went back out the door.

Winnie wandered for a little while longer, not sure where she was going. All she knew was that she didn't want to sleep in her cold, lonely room. She considered camping in the basement, even the bathroom or the hall. Finally, when she was ready to pass out on her feet, she went back downstairs and crawled onto the lobby sofa. She pulled the bedspread up over her head and went to sleep.

* * *

Winnie thought she was dreaming.

She felt someone touch her hair, then nudge her shoulder. She felt the heavy bedspread weighing down on her and the scratchy upholstery of the sofa underneath her cheek. She wasn't sure where she was or what was going on.

"Winnie, why are sleeping out here?"

Winnie grumbled and turned over, keeping her eyes shut. Then she felt the pounding ache in her forehead and a thick pain up and down her right leg. She saw the red truck come speeding through the red light and heard the violent sound of breaking glass. She thought about Lauren and Travis, Josh and Thanksgiving, and felt like she never wanted to wake up again.

"Win, I thought you were going home."

When Winnie realized that it was Josh's voice, she decided that she was still safely asleep. She smiled a little and wound the bedspread more tightly around herself. She wanted to stay in her dream, because she knew that was the only place in her life now where Josh was likely to appear.

His voice drifted into her head again. "Win, what's going on? I was asleep and somebody pounded on my door a few times. I tried to ignore it and go back to sleep, but I just tossed and turned for a long time. So I finally got up to go downstairs and get something to drink. Was that you who pounded on my door?"

Winnie opened her eyes a crack. She didn't want the dream to end, but she was getting confused. And she was remembering even more of what had happened that night. She was remembering her cold room and Melissa's models and curling up on the lobby couch. She turned over and every detail came rushing back; she knew that this was no dream anymore.

She was looking right at Josh.

Josh was crouched next to the sofa wearing sweatpants and a big, faded rugby shirt. His eyes were full of concern and his earring glistened in the harsh lobby light. Outside it was pitch black.

"It was me that knocked on your door," Winnie said. "I'm sorry. I shouldn't have woken you up."

"Why did you knock?" Josh asked.

Winnie shook her head. She had little energy left for anything but the truth. "I wanted to see you. I wanted to know that you won't hate me forever. I wanted another chance, even though I know I just blew the last chance I'll ever have with you."

Josh looked thoughtful. He very lightly touched the bandage on Winnie's head. "Are you going to tell me what happened?"

Winnie was silent.

"Or are you one of those girls who does mysterious, self-destructive things and makes guys guess. Boy, I hope not."

Winnie wondered if she was self-destructive. Her mother had once hinted that Winnie had self-destructive tendencies, and Winnie had certainly done almost everything possible to destroy her romance with Josh. But she didn't want to be self-destructive. In spite of her kookiness, her impulsiveness, her boy craziness, and her showy clothes, she wanted to be self-reliant, happy, and sane. "I hope not, too."

"So what is the story with you, Winnie? I cannot figure you out."

"I'm not all that complicated," Winnie heard herself admit. "I probably try to come off more exotic and complex than I really am. I just don't think sometimes and I get carried away and then I try to cover up for myself and I just make things worse."

Josh softened. "Is that what happened tonight?"

"Kind of." Winnie took a deep breath. "What happened tonight is that this guy that I was involved with when I was in Europe last summer is in town, and I had a date with him tonight, too. And that's pretty much what happened the other time I stood you up—well, actually I didn't stand you up, I was just late. He called just as I was leaving and you know how I talk." She sighed. "Like right now. I should shut up while I'm ahead. I just keep getting myself in deeper and deeper."

"It's okay to talk, Win. Maybe if we'd talked a little more, some of the weirdness between us wouldn't have happened."

Winnie looked at him. There was a smile on his handsome face and a soft warmth in his eyes. He put his hand out in a formal handshake. She tentatively stuck her hand out, too. They shook.

"Hi," he whispered.

"Hi."

For a while they looked into one another's eyes.

"So what do we do now?" Winnie asked. "Since there is all this weirdness between us?"

Josh shrugged. "Maybe we should start with Thanksgiving. My folks are out of the country. I have a couple of friends I could visit. Want to come along? We could have Thanksgiving in a McDonald's along the road."

Winnie smiled. "I was supposed to be home for an early dinner tomorrow, but I missed the bus and now I'll never make it in time. Gee, maybe we should stay here and have leftover hot dogs in the student union."

"I think tomorrow even the student union will be closed." Suddenly Josh's eyes brightened. "Maybe I could drive you home in the morning. Jacksonville isn't very far."

"Two hours by car." Winnie wrinkled up her nose. "And you don't have a car."

"Mikoto flew home. He left his car keys and said I could feel free to use them."

"I don't know," Winnie said. "Does Mikoto own a BMW?"

Josh shook his head. "Mikoto drives a 1978 Dodge Dart."

Winnie laughed. "You could join us for Thanksgiving dinner. It's at my friend KC's parents' restaurant. I'm sure they wouldn't mind another person. They're "the more, the merrier" kind of folks."

"That kind of folks I like."

Winnie sat back on the couch and gazed at him. "You'd really want to come to Jacksonville with me?"

"I really would. I'd like to meet your crazy family."

"It's just my mom and she's very, very sane."

"Well, there goes that expectation." Josh sat on the sofa next to her and ran his hand down the side of her face. "I would like to know more about you, crazy Winnie. I'd like not to think of you as mysterious or flaky. I'd like to trust you and find out just what makes you tick."

He put his arms around Winnie, and she felt like she was floating on cotton candy. "I'd like that, too."

They came together at the same time for a short kiss, then stayed together for longer kisses, never sure when one kiss ended and the next one began. Finally Josh stretched out beside her on the sofa and she fell asleep while he cradled her in his arms.

Fifteen

lasses started up again on Monday. To Winnie it felt like she was starting the whole semester over. Midterms would be graded and returned soon, but finals were still a long way off. Term-paper topics had been chosen and approved. Her dorm room had been professionally cleaned and was as neat as it had been when she'd first moved in. Even the fall sky and the view of the mountains surrounding the campus had a crisp, new clarity.

In spite of Winnie's feelings of renewal and hope, she still had a few unpleasant details to take care of. After a breakfast of sweet rolls at the commons, and before French language lab, she had to take Lauren down to Mac's Foreign Auto to look at what was left of Lauren's car.

"Thanksgiving was great," Winnie babbled as they got off the downtown bus. She wasn't quite ready to deal with Lauren's reaction when they found the heap of banged-up metal that had been a classy, expensive status symbol. Winnie had planned to prepare Lauren for the grim reality, then lost her nerve and softened the story a little.

Lauren followed Winnie off the bus. Lauren was still acting preoccupied and a little sad. Her light hair squiggled loosely around her face and she wore her wire-rimmed glasses. She seemed to be intentionally dressed down in a big black sweater, faded denim skirt, leather sandals, and thick, lumpy socks. "So you all had a good time?"

"The three of us had a great time. The food at The Windchime was fantastic—of course—and the company was even better than the meal."

Lauren stared straight ahead.

"Then after Thanksgiving day was over," Winnie chattered, "Faith and KC, and I saw some movies and shopped till we dropped and then met some of our old friends, who were very impressed with how sophisticated we've all become." Winnie made a face where she spread her mouth with her thumbs, crossed her eyes, and stuck out her tongue. "Especially me."

Lauren almost smiled.

"I really wish you would have come with us," Winnie continued as she led the way past a K mart and a parking garage. They passed a street lined with rented storage units and automotive supply stores. "There was so much food left over that KC's dad sent each of us home with a big, biodegradable doggie bag. My mom didn't cook all weekend."

"It's wonderful that Josh was able to drive you home so you could get there on time," Lauren mentioned with halfhearted enthusiasm.

"You can say that again."

"How long did Josh end up staying in Jacksonville?"

"Not long." Winnie knew that Lauren was still upset over Dash, and she didn't want to throw her own joy in Lauren's face. Nonetheless, she was unable to contain her delight. As they kept on walking toward the car-repair shop, Winnie thought back to the drive down to Jacksonville.

During the two-hour drive home, Winnie and Josh had talked about *everything*. They'd discussed orientation week, and the crazy toga dance, and the misunderstanding that had come up between them after Winnie passed out in his room. They'd talked about the missed signals after that. Winnie had even told Josh all about Travis, including, of course, that she and Travis were history and that Travis would probably be gone by the time they got back to school after Thanksgiving break. The only future Travis would have in Winnie's life, she'd assured Josh, was in years to come when she would listen to his songs on the radio.

The best thing about all that talking, Winnie had realized, was the way it cleared the air. Her mother always said that communication and honesty were the foundation of good relationships, and Winnie knew now that her mom was right.

Josh had even told Winnie a few things. He'd told her how he'd moved around a lot growing up as a military brat, and how he was wary of getting tied down. He'd talked about liking computers, but not wanting to get stuck in a stuffy job. And he'd told her about his old high school girlfriend, who sounded as wild and unpredictable as Winnie.

"Josh left Jacksonville Thanksgiving night," Winnie told Lauren as they finally rounded a corner and the sign identifying Mac's Foreign Auto came into view. "He drove over to Montrose to visit this old high school teacher he really liked. After that he went to see a friend in Cotter Valley, and on Sunday he drove back here."

"How do you know he did all that?" Lauren asked, craning her neck as they walked up the driveway of the repair shop. "I didn't see Josh at breakfast this morning."

Winnie blushed. "I haven't seen him since we got back either, but he called me at home Friday, Saturday, and Sunday night, just to talk and tell me what was going on."

"That's nice." Lauren said sadly. "I haven't talked to Dash at all since I left for vacation. Not a word. I think it's hopeless."

"I'm sorry."

"Don't be sorry, Win," Lauren sighed. "It wasn't your fault."

"Maybe not." Winnie led the way inside a small office building. "But I have a feeling that in another minute, I'm going to feel like saying sorry for lots of things that aren't my fault."

They approached the counter. A man with oil-stained hands and arms was hunched over a crossword puzzle. He wore a grimy shirt with a patch on it that identified him as Tim.

"Hello, Tim," said Winnie.

Tim looked up and scowled.

Winnie leaned over the counter. "I had an accident in a white BMW on Wednesday night," she explained. "The tow truck left it here. This is the owner. Lauren, meet Tim. Tim, meet Lauren. Anyway, Tim, Lauren would like the grim news. She wants to see her car."

Tim stared at Winnie as if she were nuts. Then he yelled out his back door, "Where's the sardine can BMW?" and then went back to his puzzle.

Winnie tried to laugh.

A moment later a younger fellow in an orange jumpsuit appeared and directed the girls to a big paved area behind the office.

"Here you are, ladies," the fellow said.

Lauren stared at her car with wide, stunned eyes. There was no mistaking the personalized L.T.S. license plate, although the rest of the vehicle was not so easy to recognize. One whole side was smashed in, and two of the windows were shattered meshes of safety glass. The front bumper was bent like a pipe cleaner, and the door was crumpled like tin foil.

Lauren gasped at the extent of the damage.

"I know," Winnie peeped.

"Winnie, I can't believe you weren't more seriously hurt."

Winnie touched her forehead. The bandage was off, but the cut still stung and pulled. Winnie had brushed her bangs over it. Her limbs were spotted with bruises, and her neck was still sore. "Like I said, I'm sorry forever."

For a while Lauren stared at the car. She walked all the way around it. Then she shrugged and came back to stand by Winnie's side. "Oh well. I never liked that car all that much anyway."

"Really?"

Lauren smiled. "Of course it's a great car, but it was just one more thing that made me feel spoiled and different from everybody else. Driving it was like wearing a badge with *RICH* written across it."

"I never thought of it like that," Winnie said.

"You know, I had an okay Thanksgiving, too," Lauren added. "I went to my uncle's, who I haven't seen since I was about five. I didn't remember him, and I thought he'd be just like my mother."

"Was he?"

Lauren shook her head. "He kept telling me how my parents were too into money and social position, and that I'd done the right thing by leaving the Tri Betas and standing up for what I believed in. That made me feel less crummy about Dash."

"Well, sometimes less crummy is what it's all about."

Lauren nodded.

"What are you going to do about the car?" Winnie asked.

Lauren stood tall. "I'll call my insurance company and the car will get fixed. Then I'm going to sell it, buy some old clunker, and use the leftover money to pay my tuition and my dorm fees."

"You are?"

"That's what my uncle and I figured out. That way, even if my parents never give me another penny, at least I can stay in school for this year and next. I can do what I think is right for me."

"That sounds great," Winnie said encouragingly. She stared back at the mangled car. "Could you really support yourself through sophomore year just by selling that BMW? That must be one expensive car."

"Everything my parents give me is expensive," Lauren said. "And every expensive thing has expensive strings attached."

Lauren was feeling better than "less crummy" by the time she got back to Coleridge Hall that afternoon. She still hadn't made any progress with Dash—she hadn't even *seen* Dash—but for the moment she could put her heartache on the back burner, because a few other things were looking up in her life.

She'd been handed back her first midterm, in English Lit, and she'd gotten an A. Her and Dash's article was out in the new edition of the U of S *Weekly Journal,* and Lauren liked the way it read. Plus, she'd decided that everything her uncle had told her was true. Without money from her parents, she was finally free. It was her parents' money and their pressure to join the Tri Beta sorority that had mucked up her life in the first place. If she'd never had to rush the sorority, she never would have met Christopher Hammond, which might have meant that she never would have made a mess of it with Dash. Number three was always the zinger.

Lauren took the accident report and went downstairs to use the basement phone. She had to call the insurance company and figured she might be on for a long time. She passed the washing machines and waved to some art majors from her floor who were setting up a huge tapestry for an upcoming exhibit. Lauren set her papers up by the telephone and took out her phone credit card. Then she realized that the insurance company was local and managed to find a quarter instead. She plunked the quarter in the slot and pressed the numbers.

"All Safe Auto Insurance," answered a bright female voice. "May I help you?"

"Yes. Um, I'd like to report an accident. I'm insured by you. My friend was driving when the accident happened, though. Is that still okay?"

"No problem. It's the car that's insured, not the driver. We'll take care of everything. Now just give me your policy number and the date of your accident, and I'll start to file your claim."

Lauren gave the information, then watched the tapestry hangers while the insurance woman put her on hold.

The woman came back on. "Ms. Turnbell-Smythe?" she said.

"Yes."

"When did you say your accident occurred?"

"Last Wednesday."

"I see." Her tone of voice had changed. She sounded much tighter, even a little concerned. "I'm afraid we have a problem."

"Oh?"

"I'm afraid that your insurance policy was canceled the day before your accident occurred."

Lauren almost dropped the telephone. "What!"

"I'm sure of it," the lady explained. "It says here that this policy was purchased by a Mrs. Turnbell-Smythe to cover a four-door BMW sedan that would be driven by her daughter, Lauren. Is this Lauren?"

"Yes."

"Lauren, I'm sorry to be the one to tell you this, but it appears that your mother called last Tuesday and asked us to cancel your policy as of that very day. I remember now that I took the call. She sounded quite angry. Still, I can't believe she wouldn't have told you."

Lauren felt faint. There had been several messages to call her mother after Lauren had told her that she had been kicked out of the Tri Betas. But Lauren hadn't returned the calls, because she hadn't wanted to listen to her mother's threats and manipulations. Now she realized that her mother hadn't been calling to offer idle threats. She'd been calling to tell Lauren that she'd already laid down the law.

"Are you still there?" the insurance woman checked.

"Yes," Lauren said after a moment. "So, does that mean that I can't get any of the damage covered? You won't pay for anything?"

"I'm afraid not. Now, if the accident wasn't your fault—or rather, your friend's fault—then the other driver's policy should cover you."

Lauren heaved a huge sigh of relief.

"Thank you for calling All Safe," the woman said in closing. "I wish I could have given you better news."

After Lauren hung up, she almost called her mother in London, but she stopped herself. She wasn't going to be defeated that easily. The other driver's insurance would pay for fixing her car, and then she would still do exactly as her uncle had advised. She would sell the BMW and use the money to stay at U of S with Dash and the newspaper, and Winnie and Faith and KC and the other things in life that she truly cared about.

Sixteen

"UGH!"

KC managed to climb up the flight of stairs to her single room in her all-girls study dorm. She had lugged a huge suitcase, an overnight bag, and a shopping bag, mostly full of what her mother termed "vitals from home"—otherwise known as leftovers, vitamins, homemade skirts, and books on reducing stress—all of which KC would toss as soon as she had some free time.

"Whew!" KC muttered as she trudged her stuff the final fifty feet down the dark, quiet hallway. Most everyone seemed to be back from vacation, and she could see them through open doors, writing, reading, typing, drafting, and studying. KC was glad to be back and looked forward to catching up on her studies, too. It had been great being with her family, great being back in Jacksonville, but now KC felt like yelling, *Bring on the future!*

"Keys, keys. Where are you keys?" KC said as she reached down into her pockets.

She found them and unlocked her door, almost stepping on three envelopes that had been slipped underneath.

KC froze. She was a bit suspicious about notes. Maybe it was a reaction to the dorm mail person job she'd had to take to pay off her credit card. Or maybe she was simply being paranoid, but KC didn't feel like reading unsolicited letters. She wondered who they were from. All of the handwriting looked fussy, with curlicues and smily-faced dots. KC took a breath and bent down to pick up a pink envelope. A faint scent of perfume made its way up her nose.

"This is weird," she said to herself as she put her fingers under the flap and tore back the paper. A single page of fine, crinkly notepaper slipped out into her hand. She saw large Greek letters at the top and felt sick.

"Oh God!" she said.

She almost threw the letter down. At first she

thought some sorority type was trying to get revenge on her for having the nerve to ask a sorority queen like Courtney Conner to pose in the calendar.

"That's not it!" KC said out loud. "It's Lauren's article. The newspaper. They're mad because of the paper. They found out I told Lauren about the hazing. They're blaming me because I gave her the scoop about Christopher Hammond."

KC almost balled up the letter and threw it on the floor. "NO!" she said in a strong voice.

KC folded back the page and began reading:

Dear KC:

You may be surprised to get this note. We simply want to congratulate you on your marvelous photograph in Matthew Kallander's Classic Calendar. Frankly, we think they are some of the most stunning pictures of a coed we have ever seen. You must be so proud!

We'd love to have you over to tea and hear about your experience working on the calendar. Have you thought of a modeling career? We would love to know and would also relish any health and beauty tips you could pass on.

All the best,
The Gammas

KC looked at the note. She blinked. She turned it upside down, then she put it back into the envelope and picked up another letter.

Dearest Kahia Cayanne:
  Hello!
  We've never met you before. We don't know if you had the opportunity to rush last fall, but if you did we made a mistake by not getting in touch with you sooner. We think your photographs in the upcoming Classic Calendar are FANTAS-TIC!!!
  Quite frankly, you are the talk of our sorority. Would you be at all interested in discussing the possibility of joining our spring rush? We'd like to invite you to dinner this week on December 2nd. It will be an all-sorority occasion with the guest of honor, YOU!
  Could you please, please come!
  We'll call Monday to find out.

                              Thanx,
                              Epsi Phis

KC trembled. Was this a joke?

She dropped the letter and picked up the final note. Her hands were shaky, but in one quick stroke she had the envelope torn open and the sheet of stationery in her hand. She read once more.

> *Dear KC:*
>
> *We want to congratulate you.*
>
> *We are all of us absolutely stunned after seeing your photograph for the new campus calendar. You look elegant, gorgeous, and sophisticated. In short, it shows you off as we know you to be.*
>
> *We know the truth always comes through in pictures. That's why we are ashamed of ourselves. We had the opportunity to make you a full-fledged pledge last fall, and through misunderstanding and ignorance, we let that opportunity slip by.*
>
> *I will call you about this personally this week. I would also like you to go shopping with me. From the photos I know that I could use your beauty and clothes advice. Looking forward to it.*
>
> *Courtney Conner*

KC was suddenly dizzy. Her heart was pounding, and her breath was short. What was she going to do?

"Look at this, Josh," Winnie said later that same afternoon.

"Look at what, Win. I'm looking at you."

"Well, here's looking at you, too. Oh, wait"—Winnie giggled—"wrong classic movie."

Winnie and Josh were lounging in his room, arms around one another, while Mikoto was putting up some new posters he'd bought on his visit home. Winnie and Josh stretched out on the floor amidst a pile of books and floppy disks. Ragtime piano music played on Josh's tape machine, and a cool breeze made his window curtains flap.

"See," Winnie said, "this is the calendar I told you about, the one KC and that weirdo in my film class made."

Josh leaned over and pretended to draw a mustache on KC's upper lip. "Hey, Mikoto," Josh joked, "maybe you should put this up instead of posters of race cars."

Mikoto, who had glasses and wore jeans and a polo shirt, turned and looked at KC's photo with approval. "Is that supposed to be Katharine Hepburn?"

"Yes!" Winnie cried. "You got it!"

Josh borrowed the mock-up calendar and flipped through it. "This looks pretty good."

Winnie watched him, until he caught her staring. Then she leaned over and kissed him. "Everything looks pretty good all of sudden. The grass. The sky. Your computer. My bruises and scrapes. The turkey à la king in the dining commons."

Josh started to tickle her gently, which made Winnie pretend to be in pain long enough for him to let down his defenses so she could dive in and tickle him back.

"Would you two act like college freshmen?" Mikoto demanded. "We're getting midterms back this week. Term papers still have to be written. You're both acting much too happy."

"That's because Josh is a demented technonerd, and I'm still an undeclared major," Winnie told Mikoto. "So if I flunk a class, maybe I can decide that it really wasn't something I needed for my degree anyway."

Mikoto hammered in another tack. "I wonder if I can have an undeclared major and still become a doctor."

Josh thought for a moment. "Why don't you try it?"

"I don't think so," Mikoto cracked.

"You pre-med types are way too intense," Winnie teased. "You're all going to get ulcers. Melissa's the same way."

"Hey, Win," Josh decided. "Maybe we should fix Mikoto and Melissa up."

Mikoto shook his head. "Nah. Roommates going out with roommates. It's like double-dating in high school. Very dangerous."

"You think so?"

"The only thing worse is a pre-med going out with another pre-med."

Winnie smiled at Mikoto. "I think Melissa may be taken anyway. She went to Thanksgiving at the house of this guy I know from high school, and I guess she had a good time. Not that she told me all the gory details. Melissa's kind of the keep-things-inside type, as opposed to the I'll-tell-any-one-who'll-listen type, like you know who."

"Who?" Josh laughed.

"Beats me. Anyway, Melissa was in a very good mood this morning. That's all I can say."

"Oh well, Mikoto," said Josh.

Mikoto shook his head. "I guess my old high school girlfriend will still have to put up with me."

"Poor girl."

"Okay," Winnie finally conceded, standing up and tucking KC's calendar under her arm. "I'm going to act like a college freshman and get a start on my dreaded Western Civ book report."

Josh held up his hands as if he were warding off Dracula, grabbed Winnie for one last kiss, and then pushed her toward the door. "Go on. I have to work on a term paper, too. Let's meet for dinner?"

Winnie saluted.

He kissed the top of her head. "See you then."

"You will."

"I can't wait."

"Me either. Have a good computer class. Go, be a nerd."

Josh kissed her again, and Winnie jogged out his door.

She practically floated down the hallway, she was feeling so good. For a while she'd hated the idea of having Josh live right down the hall, but now that things were working out, she loved the everyday playfulness and closeness that living in the same dorm gave to her and Josh's relationship. They could get together for late-night study sessions, breakfasts, junk-food binges, and video games. They could get to know one another in a deep, relaxed, real way.

"Coed dorms," Winnie sang, "I love you."

The door to her room was cracked open, and Winnie remembered that she hadn't bothered to lock it when she'd gone down the hall to visit Josh. "Hi Mel," she called as she entered. She sensed that someone was inside and was glad to have a chance to show off KC's calendar. Plus, no matter how tight-lipped Melissa tried to be, Winnie was dying to find out all the details of her Thanksgiving in Jacksonville with Brooks.

Winnie held the calendar up with a grin and strode into her room. But as soon as she took a step inside, her stomach seemed to fall to her shoes and the cut on her head began to throb. She lunged back and pulled the door closed behind her.

Travis turned around and gazed at her.

"I thought you'd be gone by now," Winnie gasped.

Travis held up his hands. "Hi beautiful. I decided that you're right. I'm too impulsive. Man, I haven't given us a chance. I missed you so much over the last four days. And I have great news. The Beanery hired me for a regular gig, so I'm going to stay in Springfield for a while longer and see if we can work things out."

Winnie sank onto her bed and didn't say a word.

Here's a sneak preview of
Freshman Games, *the sixth
book in the absorbing story of*
FRESHMAN DORM.

"So then I had to go and tell Lauren the bad news about her BMW. I mean, she took it really well, but what a drag for her. I was totally bummed to find out that the guy who hit me wasn't insured."

"Winnie, do you have to talk about this right now? It's not exactly good for sales."

"Relax, KC. The calendars are selling themselves. Anyway, this morning, before I called the insurance company, I was in the best mood of my entire life. Josh and I had the greatest time last night, and it wasn't even some heavy romantic thing. I mean, there were moments that were heavy and romantic and wonderful and all that, but mostly we talked nonstop."

"You mean, *you* talked nonstop," KC interrupted.

Winnie grinned. "We hung out in the dorm and then at four in the morning we hitched a ride in the back of this guy's pickup to the top of Wimer Mountain. We sat there with our arms around each other and watched the sun rise."

KC shrugged.

Winnie had a dreamy expression. "Of course I'll probably snore through my history class, but I think it was the best night of my entire life. I'm going to ask Josh to Winter Formal, even though I don't usually go to corny events like that. But Josh is so great, and our relationship is so great that even something as weird as Winter Formal will be great, too."

"How can you say Winter Formal is weird?" KC said to Winnie. "From what I've heard it's the biggest social even on campus." KC paused to smile and wave at someone she recognized. "All the sorority and fraternity members go to Winter Formal."

Winnie rolled her eyes. "KC, I can't believe you're talking about sororities again. I thought you were through with that stuff."

KC tensed. "And I thought you were through with Travis Bennett."

Winnie took a moment to respond. "I am," she

finally insisted. "It's not my fault he hasn't left town yet."

"Does Josh know that Travis is still around?" KC asked.

"He doesn't know yet," Winnie admitted. "But he will. I'll tell him. Soon." She turned away from KC and neatened a stack of calendars. "Faith, you think that's okay, don't you, that I haven't told Josh about Travis yet?"

For once Faith didn't jump in and play referee, making sure that their old trio was still getting along. KC had good reason to question Winnie. But Faith sensed that KC's irritation wasn't really over Winnie's truthlessness, but over Winnie's glowing happiness with Josh. KC might be the most glamorous freshman on campus, but, unlike Winnie, she wasn't in love. She didn't even have a date for Winter Formal.

Still, Faith didn't comment on her friends' motives. She didn't tell Winnie to be truthful or insist that KC keep her head. For once, Faith preferred to hand out calendars and think about the color of Alice's apron and whether the White Rabbit should scamper or hop.

"Who's that?" Winnie gasped, grabbing the edge of the table and letting her mouth fall open.

KC's mouth fell open, too.

Faith stared. A tall, dark-haired young man was

walking up to their table. He wore a heavy sweater that matched his pleated wool slacks. He wasn't just good looking. Faith recognized him instantly from the calendar.

"Oh, it's Warren Manning," KC blurted.

"Mr. December," Winnie giggled.

"He's even more gorgeous in person than he is in his picture," Faith whispered.

Warren came up to the table and offered KC a brilliant paper-white smile, "Hello, ladies. How are sales?"

"Even better than we expected," KC managed in a semicool voice. "And how are you?"

"Terrific."

Faith was amazed. When things got hot, KC seemed to get even cooler. Faith didn't have time to think about guys right now, but she could never have chatted casually with Warren. Even madly-in-love Winnie still stood there with her mouth open.

Warren, however, wasn't interested in Faith or Winnie. His eyes were on KC. He extended a hand to shake. "You're KC Angeletti. We met briefly during the photo shoot."

"Did we?"

"I'm Warren Manning."

KC nodded, as if she'd really needed a reminder.

Warren still held KC's hand. "I guess you're not only the beauty behind this, you're the brains, too."

KC stood taller, even cooler and more composed. "I guess so."

Shoppers nudged Warren, trying to get to the table to buy more calendars. He shifted and leaned toward KC. "I admired your photo, and when I saw you here, I came by to say hello."

"Did you?" KC challenged.

He smiled and acknowledged the crowd. "But I guess this isn't a great place to get acquainted. Why don't you give me your phone number? I'd like to get together sometime."

KC pretended to consider his suggestion for a moment. Finally, with Faith and Winnie staring like idiots, she wrote her number on a sales receipt and handed it to him. "There you are. Maybe we can get together and talk about the calendar."

"Among other things." Warren looked at the number, then stuck it in his pocket. He winked at KC. "Thanks. I'll give you a call sometime."

"You do that."

"I will."

KC maintained her cool composure until Warren had made his way back through the crowd and disappeared. As soon as he was gone, she faced Faith and Winnie.

For the first time that morning, the trio was perfectly in tune. At the exact same moment, Faith, KC, and Winnie put their hands to their faces, came together in a huddle, and screamed.